"Much like the Charlie Parker riff tune of the same name, Larry Strauss' new jazz novel, Now's The Time is punchy, energetically fast-paced and fun! The narrative brings the reader as close as one can get to the sometimes gritty lifestyle, lingo and humanity of the jazz musician, without actually being one. Following the exploits of central character Didi Heron, a young female jazz trumpeter desperately in search of her long-deceased father's true legacy and spirit via a missing tape of his final gig made just prior to his fatal car accident, the plot takes the twists and turns of a masterful bebop solo and brings the reader and characters on a journey of true self-discovery. Drawing inspiration from a potpourri of stories from our illustrious American jazz tradition, notably the triumph and tragedy of clean-living trumpeter Clifford Brown who perished in a car accident in 1956, Strauss has created a moving work of fiction rooted in historical fact. I wholeheartedly recommend this warm, witty and passionate book!"
—Alan Hood, Associate Professor, University of Denver, and noted historian on Clifford Brown.

"Larry Strauss really knows how to tell a lively story, just like the great improvisers he celebrates. Now's the Time avoids every cliché of jazz fiction. Its main character searches for a legendary recording and finds her self in the process. Didi Heron's view from the bandstand is sharp, accurate, unsentimental. She became as real to me as Clifford Brown or Mary Lou Williams. More, please!"
—Michael Steinman, host of *Jazz Lives*: www.jazzlives.wordpress.com

Now's the Time

Now's the Time

Larry Strauss

This is a work of fiction. Names, characters, places, and incidents are products of the author's imagination or are used fictitiously and are not to be construed as real. Any resemblance to actual events, locales, organizations, or persons, living or dead, is entirely coincidental.

ISBN: 0-9723706-7-6
Library of Congress Control Number: Pending

Kearney Street Books
Now's the Time
First KSB printing (May, 2010).

Printed in the United States of America

Kearney Street Books
Po Box 2021
Bellingham, WA 98227
360-738-1355
www.kearneystreetbooks.com

For Eleanor

Prologue:
Route 40 • February, 1956

The back seat seatback froze against Billy's cheek until the heat of his own face made a warm spot; then the car jerked on slick road and his face slid into arctic vinyl. Billy needed a shave. He needed a bed. His eyes burned if they stayed open but he couldn't keep them closed. Snow melted against the side windows and the dark and faded world beyond it. The car was cool and quiet inside, except for the robotic snores of Lonnie Baylor and the intermittent humming of an up-tempo *Moon River* by the woman at the wheel.

Billy got his eyes closed again and tried to fill that darkness with the face of his four-year-old daughter, Didi. He tried to picture that night two months ago when Venora brought her down to The Last Door on 52nd Street. Didi sat with her mother and then when Billy and the guys took the stage, she ran between the tables and threw herself up on Billy's lap. Billy hadn't known what to do at first. He'd started to lift her off and send her away, but he couldn't do that. She owned that lap, and as Lonnie counted into the first tune, Billy just reached around Didi's arms and played and Didi was mesmerized.

Billy tried to hold on to that image, but when he felt around in his memory for the music of that night, what came back to him instead was the music of two hours ago. He couldn't stop hearing it or feeling it at the tips of his frozen fingers.

Just a few more nights now: Philly, then Camden, Trenton, then back home for a month or two—or however long it took to lay down the tracks for the next two albums. Billy thought maybe he'd take Didi with him to the studio. Let her keep the engineer company if that was all right.

A new thumping beneath the car said, *One, two, one-two-three-four*. Broke the quiet like Lonnie's finger-popping when he set the quintet into motion. But this was not a good sound. Then from outside somewhere a metallic shriek, then quiet.

Time stretched out.

Billy was spinning. A sharp glow and darkness swirled together like whipped cream and dark cherry syrup in a blender. Lonnie's head went over the top of the front seat and into Billy's chest, and he said, *Hey!*

The woman at the wheel screamed *No!* Then *Lord!*

Then everything went upside down. The smell of blood pinched Billy's nose. A dull pain made him close his eyes. When he opened them again his vision was scrambled. The steering wheel was a halo over Lonnie's head.

Billy felt his body leaving the car. A moment later he was waist-deep in clean snow. Wind made the trees tremble slightly. Billy stopped feeling tired. The snowfall and the branches above his head and the evening sounds were beautiful. But other things were not. A hubcap was a few feet from his head, and a door, and just beyond that, wrapped around a highway guard rail was half of the car, the green Plymouth they'd been riding in.

He looked around for Lonnie and the woman. He thought he could see part of her in one half of the car and part of her in the other. He spotted one of LB's shoes, then saw an arm hanging over the passenger side door and a hat upside down catching a snow drift. Billy tried to go back to his thoughts. The Last Door. His daughter. *Didi Pancake,* he sometimes called her.

Chapter One:
NYC • Spring, 1976

Morningside Drive

My name is Didi Heron and I play the trumpet, and for me, few things are as depressing as the last night of a gig. Maybe it wasn't that way back in my father's day, but to quote Bud Powell: "The scene changes." All the clubs along 52nd Street are gone now, replaced by ugly towers of glass and steel and restaurants I can't afford. Not too many jazz clubs left in the city and most of them want fusion bands, jazz rock with electric bass and guitar and drums all over the stage, people dancing in front like they just dropped some LSD. Or that freeform stuff, dudes wailing on horns and slamming pianos in the seventy-two tone vortex. So those of us still trying to play bebop—innovating on a smaller scale, one bar at a time—know all about the closing night blues.

Which makes it important to appreciate the little things. The small marquee with Didi Heron Quartet in slightly lopsided black letters above my glossy headshot, my fro thick and round and full the way it hardly ever really is.

When I came through the squat front doorway of Benet's Night Spot—at 5′8″ it's like entering a mouse hole of music and smoke—Eddie the bartender waved me over. Four dudes faced him at the bar. They were slurping the hard stuff like they needed straws. Eddie was setting up glasses. "Somebody called for you," he said. "Guy from Ala-something Records."

"Alamode?" One of the only bop labels left, but to Eddie just another cocktail and some chump change in the tip jar.

"That's right. Alamode. Like ice cream on pie."

"What was his name?" I asked.

"Didn't say. Just wanted to know if you were playing here. I said this was your last night. Then he wanted to know what time the first set got started and if he needed a reservation. I told him not to worry."

"Great," I said.

"Can you play?" asked one of the cats at the bar. He took a lusty drag on his cigarette, made the smoke hook up into his nose.

"Man, she all right," one of his pals said, stuffing tobacco into a corn cob pipe, lighting it with a wooden match. "I caught her set the other night. She halfway decent." He chuckled. "Got a boy on piano can play his ass off!"

Like I care what these dudes think. I gave them my back. Like Miles. You knew he paid no mind to the peanut gallery. Miles Dewey Davis played for himself and perhaps for some higher musical authority. That's how you've got to be. Like my "boy" Derrick—and he *does* play his ass off. I knew that from the start. We met at The Bridgeport Jazz Festival. I was with the City College Jazz Band that night and we were up first, to get things swinging while the parking lot filled and people found chairs or rocks to sit on. Everyone in the band was pumped and played loud—and probably drowned out my one solo—but it didn't matter, because after we finished I got to hear Ella caress the air and Joe Pass make sparks fly off his guitar. Got to catch Lucky Thompson, Johnny Griffin, and Zoot Sims trading fours and then Woody Shaw blowing a tribute to Louis Armstrong.

Later on, while dudes in overalls broke down speakers and amplifiers, one slender guy with dreads and a kaleidoscopic earring sat in front of the baby grand on which Tommy Flanagan and George Cables had taken turns. I figured the guy for an electrician or a tuner. Until he started to play. First with just the left hand, a blues line. Then a crazy chromatic right-hand thing, up-tempo and a little ahead of itself. It made me have to unpack my horn and jam with him. I knew the tune but couldn't place it until he started this euphonic hum and a weird, muted cry, and I realized it was the Tadd Dameron line, *Mating Call.*

It seemed to impress him that I knew it.

We played for an hour and I missed my bus back to the city. We played *A Night in Tunisia* very slow, then *Autumn in New York* very fast, and after that we just played, a harmonic conversation and for the first time in my life I felt the music coming not from my lips but from somewhere deep.

He drove me back to the city in his battered Midget and I gave him my phone number. We got to dueting regularly and things got intense. We played professionally, here and there, mostly in bars where people tried to talk over the music and sometimes shut up if we played with enough command. Good training. Paying our dues. The money, of course, was shit. But it seemed now like our hard work was about to pay off.

Derrick had been late before—but never this late. Eddie was cool about letting me use the bar phone, so I called Derrick's crib but got no answer. At about 9:15 the crowd murmur had the sour buzz of impatience and the owner of the club told me to get my ass up on the stage. He dimmed the lights and announced the Didi Heron *Trio*. I took the stage with my bassist Terrance and my drummer George.

Our first tune was that Tadd Dameron line Derrick and I had first played together. *Mating Call* felt strange without the emphatic chords from Derrick's steady hands, but I saw smiles in the audience and took that to mean that I was, to quote Gershwin, doing all right. Until I took my solo. Then I knew I was shaking the air in the wrong direction, making background music to the thoughts of a glazed audience. Our second tune, *Speak Low*, seemed to be an invitation to people at some back tables to do just that, their chatter overcome, briefly, by some dishes breaking in the kitchen. Nothing that would have even fazed Pops or Fats or Diz or LB or Miles and I guess it wouldn't have bothered me much if I could have coaxed a little rapture from my horn. When that happens the world inside the club stops, mouths shut, ears open, the dishes show respect.

But my chops just weren't getting it. I spoke low on *Speak Low* and remained earthbound on *Star Eyes*. Then on Derrick's original, *Pulmonary Artery*, I flexed my lungs and my frustration but it felt like all show, no passion coming through. Hank Mobley's *Uh Huh* sounded more like *Uh-Uh*. And *Morningside Drive*, the one composition my father ever wrote, his *letter*—as cats back then used to call an original melody—which was supposed to transport that dude from Alamode Records and the rest of the audience to someplace special...Well, it ended up just a colorless melody in G-minor.

When the first set was over, and light applause dissolved, I tried to sneak off the stand and into the kitchen—and maybe out the back door—but I was greeted by a white guy in a Newport Jazz Festival sweatshirt. He wasn't my idea of a record executive type. More like a guy who hangs around the scene thinking he's cool. His nearly bald head caught the harsh overhead light. His voice was large and smooth.

"Ms. Heron, I'm Nils Tanner, Alamode Records." He shook my hand. "What happened to your pianist? He gonna make the second set?"

I shrugged and he blew cigarette smoke over my shoulder. At least the cat was honest. Don't pretend you're interested in what I can do when it's my punk-ass doesn't-show-up-when-I-need-him pianist and soon to be ex-boyfriend you came to hear. *But fuck you and your honesty, anyway!*

"Well," Tanner said. "So...Didi Heron. I'll be keeping an eye out for you. An ear out for you." A laugh squeezed out of his face. "Didi Heron. Good jazz name. There was a pianist, back in the fifties. Played with Lonnie Baylor until we lost LB to that awful car accident."

"Billy Heron."

"The pianist. Yes, that was his name."

"He was my father."

"No kidding."

"He died in that car, too."

"Yes, of course. I remember. I knew your father. Met him at Birdland."

"But you were really there to see Lonnie Baylor."

"Everyone wanted to see LB. And everyone wanted to play with him. Your father had a sweet situation."

"Guess you don't think much of his chops either."

Tanner smiled and stared at me, then squared his jaw, took a long drag on his cigarette, and stubbed it out in a mosaic ashtray on the bar. "Not really, if you want to know—and I guess you want to know. Your father had all kinds of technique. Had to, to hang with LB. But I always felt like Billy was holding back. Saving it for a rainy day that never came. I think you do the same thing."

"Not like you, though. You don't hold back."

"Why would I do that?" he asked and walked away, and left me there wanting to cuss him out, but what the hell for? Better yet, cuss him out on my horn in the second set. But I wasn't sure how to do it, exactly; wasn't sure how to play my own self-respect like Bird and Dizzy did at Earl Wilson when he Uncle-Tom'd them on TV. All I could do was play angry, loud. So that's what I did, and people got up to leave because they couldn't hear themselves talk. By then, I don't think Tanner was in the room anymore.

CHAPTER TWO:

YOU'VE CHANGED

Suddenly, every other part of my life became intolerable: the cruddy little apartment, my two roommates and their unwashed boyfriends and graffiti murals and crowded and funky play readings every other night spilling out the window onto the fire escape, my day job as a middle school substitute teacher taking roll and breaking up fights. Without Derrick on piano, it all lost its charm. I felt like that hitchhiker in *Five Easy Pieces* sitting in the backseat of Jack Nicholson's car complaining about all the crap, how everything was just a bunch of crap, crap and more crap.

D turned up a few days later on my answering machine, testifying to a wrong place, wrong time misunderstanding. Something about helping an old friend move from Bed-Stuy to Flatbush with a truck dragging its tail pipe that turned out to have been stolen and then lent to the friend of a friend of a friend and a traffic cop with an attitude who found some loose joints and a hash pipe in the sock drawer of a dresser they were moving. Supposedly the grass and the equipment belonged to the friend's ex-girlfriend, but Derrick and his friend had been in the wrong place at the wrong time with the wrong people before, so the judge sent the friend to Rikers and Derrick to Paragon House Rehab.

The story was so stupid it almost had to be true—but I didn't care. He shouldn't have been helping anyone move the day of the last night at Benet's when a couple of really romping sets might have got us an extension or a return date. For now there were no prospects. Terrance and George were talking about going in another direction. And that record company suit kept calling the manager at Benet's who kept calling me about getting in touch with Derrick. I was tempted to find out the Paragon House phone number and give that to him.

But not really. I just wanted to get on with things. Make some money baby-sitting junior high school badasses and get my roommate Laquarie to pay the electric bill. It was her turn and two weeks past due. I had to deal with a sticky valve on my horn. The oil wasn't doing anything. Most of all I had to stay optimistic. Even without any logical reason to, even if not giving up on music ended up being the only real accomplishment, I'd just have to make that enough, just make my heart right with it. Keep practicing, even when the neighbors pounded against my wall and floor and ceiling. Mostly they didn't—and there was the occasional applause from a window one flight up or across the alley to keep me going. But going where? No time to think about that. No time for bitterness either. I called Benet's and gave them Derrick's home phone to pass on and said, "He might be out of town for a while but keep trying."

I was ready to take life as a solo, play it in the right key, on the beat, or better yet, steps ahead.

I took my horn to Harry's Music on 9th Avenue. Harry's guy Skeeter unclogged the valve, polished the instrument, and said no charge for me. I met some dudes there picking up conga skins off the discount table and they invited me to jam with them on a rooftop on 181st Street. I think they were joking—or trying to pick me up—but I showed up there anyway, a few nights later, and we jammed standards in Afro-Caribbean time while the sun set over the great cables of the GW Bridge. A cat named Dario collected three dollars at the rooftop door from all the non-musicians, and served beer and barbecue. He passed a hat for the entertainment while we blew spontaneous salsa until after midnight. We split $38.55 six ways, but I could work with that. It wasn't about the money. Next morning I was doing geography with 8th graders at I.S. 44 thinking about another jam session that night, thinking this was it. Forget the clubs and record labels. Music was best played and heard ten floors up under the stars. I wasn't thinking about Derrick—wasn't even thinking about *thinking about* his sorry ass—until an assistant principal came into the classroom with a memo from the Board of Education, saying it was urgent. The memo said I had until Friday to turn in the renewal form for my teaching license. I had started filling it out last week and then forgot about it. Couldn't remember where I'd left it and asked for another, but the school didn't have any. Went home and couldn't find it anywhere so the next day after work, I rode the IRT to Downtown Brooklyn and waited an hour twenty at the Board of Ed's substitute office to find out I was only entitled to one form. If I wanted another I would have to request a replacement form. Budget cuts, a form shortage in this bankrupt city. I filled out the request form, waited in another line to find out I wouldn't receive it in the mail for at least ten working days (*non*-working days for me if I didn't have that form a hell of a lot sooner). Looking around the apartment again, I remembered where the stupid half-filled-out form was: at Derrick's. I went over there, forgetting that he'd changed the lock—after a robbery attempt—and now had one of those special keys that was hard to get copied. Which he'd never bothered to do. "Why would I want you to have a key when I never want to let you out of my sight?" he'd said, the last time it had come up. Now I was standing in the dim hallway cussing. I kicked the door but it didn't budge. The neighbor's dog threw a barking fit.

I was thinking about saying a simple *fuck it,* and rationalize some divine message telling me to give it up. Walk away from this Board of Ed gig and figure out something else. Like swapping major for minor in the middle of a riff. Sometimes it's just the right thing to do. Lean over the precipice just far enough to feel the fall without falling. But I guess you've got to be willing to fall, head-first, if it comes to that. And I guess I wasn't ready for that.

So I walked uptown instead. To the subway station and down into the tunnel. Hurled my body into the rush hour slam dance.

Broken street lamps made it dark when I came up out of the IRT tunnel. A row of over-grown trees made it darker still as I approached the Paragon House drug rehab, a six-story building on West 83rd Street with tall pillars at the entry and grimy men bumming cigarettes behind the big pile of garbage waiting like an orphan at the curb. One of the men said something in my direction and I thought I might have to bounce a foot off him and jam. I'd run the 220 and 440 hurdles in high school, so I can sprint and kick at the same time. But not this time—didn't have to. The front door was unlocked. No kind of security on the other side. Maybe there was a camera somewhere. I walked in and almost walked out, thinking how I didn't want to be there and had no interest in dealing with hop-heads and junkies. But right away I heard a strange melody from somewhere. A loud echo, reverberating through the place like musical thoughts in a giant head. I remembered how Charlie Parker had written *Relaxin' at Camarillo* in honor of his rehab stop during a west coast swing and how Mingus and others had paid musical tribute to Bellevue Hospital over the years and I wondered when the breathing world would be treated to, perhaps, *The Paragon House Blues*. Could I write it as a visitor? Might have been too late for that; could be I was hearing it already as the spontaneous invention of Derrick. That was definitely his forceful hand I was hearing, his energy. Although it sounded like he was playing an old toy piano.

Which he was. In a dusty rec-room, all scuffed linoleum with faded marble around the base of the floor. A caged TV played *Sanford & Son* while Derrick and three other dudes jammed hard and ridiculous, grinding a heavy funk with make-shift instruments. Derrick, sitting on a vinyl chair in a pablum-colored robe, hair naps all twisted around themselves, making the most of two toy octaves on a little piano he had on his lap. A white dude with a shaved head did a vocal funk bass line with his mouth through a cracked megaphone. Another dude worked a washboard with his fingernails and a pencil. Rounding out the lunatic quintet was an old brother squeezing syncopation out of a mop-wringer and someone's kid playing a front desk bell.

Who the hell would bring his child into this place? It smelled like toe-jam, industrial lemon, and shit. A dude across from the "quintet" was squatting on the edge of a low radiator, covering his head like the circus-sounding funk was killing him, although his feet moved like he wanted to get up and dance.

An old guy came up behind me. He had a white fro and beard, black Santa Claus in a gray jumpsuit and platform shoes. "Can I help you?" he asked.

When I didn't answer right away, he said, "I run this place."

At that point, Derrick looked up, still slapping the funk on plastic hammers, and said, "Watch it, Stan Man. That's my girl."

"I ain't nobody's girl," I said. "Least of all your sorry ass."

Some of the other guys reacted. They were laughing—at him, at me, maybe also at themselves. I doubt I was the only female who ever came up in the Paragon House and cussed a dude out. Probably heard it every day. Sorry-asses messing up lives trying to get a fix, trying to feel good in their own bodies, trying for that ultimate liberation.

"Can't have no girl no way," Stan Man said. "Not for your first three-sixty-five clean and sober."

"Ain't got no drug problem," Derrick said, and quoted, within the funk, on that silly toy piano, a little Charlie Parker *Moose the Mooch* and some Bud Powell *Un Poco Loco*. And I almost laughed, but didn't.

"What they all say," Stan Man said and he did laugh. "Bird used to say that shit. Ain't got no drug problem. Got a money problem. Got a police problem. Got a can't-remember-what-the-fuck-I-did-yesterday problem." He laughed again and it irritated me.

"What do you know about Charlie Parker?"

"Used to supply that nigga. Miles too. Prez Young. Monk. I was they main line." He said it matter-of-factly. No remorse coming through. Then he took a harmonica out of his pocket and joined in the sublimely stupid jam session, free-forming it with about half an ounce of lame-ass style and even less technique. There was something so unjust in having to listen to his no-talent blues while he had assisted so many soulful serenaders in their own demise.

I leaned in toward Derrick and said: "Hey, D, I need the keys to your pad."

He threw his head back and grunted, "You need..." Like it was all too much for him. Like I was the cause of his problems. He did me a once-over, pounding the toy piano.

"I'm not playing, man. I left a paper up in there and I need it now. Trying to keep my day job."

"So you're not my girl but you need my apartment."

"Just give me the damn key."

"I don't have it. They took everything from me when I came in here...Except my heart, which remains in your hand." In that dusty Paragon House light his eyes were iridescent gray, like those of a cat hiding under a chair.

I just stared at him and he worked a minor seventh into his disjointed toy piano vamp. I said, "Where's the damn key?"

Stan Man was still behind me. "I would just need for him to authorize me to transfer it over in your possession and you would have to sign the property release form."

"Then let's go," I said, and Stan Man Santa Claus made eye contact with Derrick who dropped his hands from the piano and nodded, sadly, and then watched me walk.

Santa took me down a hallway to a musty old office with the name Stan Duboclet on the door. He sat me in a swiveling plastic chair and put a long piece of paper in front of me. He told me to press hard so my signature would go through all the carbons. He told me to print my name below my signature, then looked at it.

"Didi Heron." He studied my face.

"Can I get the key now?" I asked.

"You're Billy Heron's kid, ain't you? I remember you at The Last Door on 52nd Street sitting on your daddy's lap."

"You gonna tell me you sold smack to my father?"

"Billy? Mister-Clean-Living himself?" He laughed. "Your pops was good people. Lonnie, too. You couldn't get them to try nothing. Smart mothafuckas. But the ax man, Felton Payne. And that woman LB was with that night—the one who crashed the car—now she was another story..."

"What are you trying to say? What are you telling me?"

"I'm just telling you like it is, kid. I made a lot of regrets for myself that I've had to make my peace with. My disease is a mothafucka. I just need to respect it and keep practicing my principles in the here and now, you dig? Helping young brothas like your boy Derrick."

"Are you telling me you killed my father?"

He gave me a hollow smile. "Hey now. That wasn't me sold that woman that shit. Like I said. My disease, her disease—and the disease always be actin' a fool. Sellin' shit, buyin' shit, usin' shit, crashin' a car. But I do take personal responsibility and I can make it up to you if you just give me a chance." He leaned forward.

"Go fuck yourself."

"Hey now." He folded his arms and tilted his head back. "We don't allow profanity on the premises." He stood, popped his fingers and a big dude in a blue uniform appeared. "She's got to go."

"I'm gone...Soon as this chump gives me that house key."

The Pinkerton looked at his boss. Duboclet sucked his gums for a second, shifted his eyes, then waved him away and opened a thick metal door behind his desk and leaned into a big vault. There was a mirror stuck to the inside of the metal door so he could keep an eye on me over his shoulder while he sifted through the junk of those stranded junkies still funking around three rooms away and otherwise lurking throughout this damp stinking old building. This guy was just another kind of pusher now. Getting cats hooked on his brand of stupid so-called wisdom and self-justification, selling them the line that they didn't have to be sorry for screwing themselves and everyone around them up. And for that he kept their money and everything else, including their self-respect and their private thoughts and dreams.

"Here go your boy's key." He turned around and handed me a tarnished 8th note with a ring of keys looped through the head. Then he locked his vault and led the way out of that place and I walked a step behind him thinking that if he tried in any way to touch any part of me with any part of him I would swing that ring of keys upside his head and knock him on his ass.

"I wasn't there just to sell junk that night."

I didn't hear him at first.

He turned. "That's right," he said. "I came to hear LB and the fellows play. Your dad, too. Man, he was tough. Always liked Billy for his lay-back style. Always. I had all their records and wanted another. Snuck a Wollensack in with me. See, I wasn't just about the junk, y'understand. It was more than that. And let me tell you somethin', your father, the last time he played, he was special good. I mean special good that night. Ain't holdin' nothin' back, like he knew it was his last night on this earth. I'm sorry to say it like that but you ain't no kid. You got to hear it like it is. Don't hide from truth."

I stopped walking and made him stop. I could see the door in the dark entryway and street light streaking through and could hear the noise of cars and street radios and the circular talk of dudes loitering on the sidewalk. I looked straight at Stan Duboclet and said, "What the *fuck* are you talking about?"

"Hey, lady, I told you. No scurrility in this domicile."

"You recorded my father's last gig?"

He made a "forgive her" gesture with his hands. "I coulda got a lot of money for that tape. Always wondered why didn't nobody ever released it. But I ain't done it for the money. I loved the LB Five. Coulda sold that fine-ass reel of magnetic magic to Buster Choles with that little underground jazz label out of Trenton. But the club manager, Clay McKee, saw my microphone and called me out and that brotha had pull all up and down the east coast. West coast, too. And he used to play linebacker for the Colts. Coulda broke me in three. So I gave him the tape. Then he wanna go and bogart my Wollensack. *Man!*"

"Where's the tape."

"Hell if I know."

"Open your vault and let me see."

He laughed. "Lady, I would have been sold it."

I didn't know what to believe. I walked away, looking straight ahead with the dread of having to pass by all those sleazy dudes on the street. Duboclet yelled after me: "I think Clay give it to LB. The tape. I don't know. I was mainly thinking bout the Wollensack. Shit belonged to my uncle and he was a mean mothafucka. Had his own Nixon tapes and shit. You take care a yo-self."

It was nearly nine o'clock when I got into Derrick's tiny apartment. I could hardly move around the place. Crates of records blocked the doorways and furniture was all pushed together in the middle of the floor, as if he was about to paint the walls and never got the paint. The place reeked of sour milk and a 40-gallon tank of algae and dead guppies which sat atop Derrick's beat-down upright piano. I stood on a chair and opened a window near the ceiling, which let in an even worse stench from garbage piled out front. I searched the cracked linoleum table where I'd started filling out that form two weeks ago. There was a box of stale Wheat Thins and next to it a pile of pornographic comic books called Super Stud and The Virginia Slims. Not Derrick's style so maybe that dumbass friend he was helping move had left them there. Or maybe it *was* Derrick's style and I was a blind fool. I just wanted to find that stupid form and get out of there. I was jumpy from footsteps in the apartment above. The phone rang and I was imagining it was a shadow girlfriend. Making me crazy for a second there. Then Derrick's answering machine kicked in and after D's thinks-he's-cool outgoing message—made absurd by the fact that he wouldn't be getting back to anyone anytime soon—I heard the too-smooth voice of that record company dude:

"This is Nils Tanner trying to reach Derrick Gamble. Hope this is the right number." Said he needed a piano for some studio sessions and tour dates and thought Derrick was the man.

I wrote down the phone number and extension Tanner left him, thinking that when I was in a better mood I might pass on the information to Derrick. I wrote it on the back of one of those ridiculous comic books and as I was tearing the corner of the page, I looked down and saw, beneath it, the damn form I'd been looking for. I snatched it off the table and turned to get the hell out of there. But then I didn't go. Not right away. I kept looking around the place. I wasn't sure what I was looking for. Maybe a reason to forgive Derrick. He wasn't a bad guy. Just foolish, really, which a reasonable person might think forgivable. But at the moment I wasn't into thinking it was right to excuse a person who squandered any part of his life for any reason. Mocking all the folks who'd ever been robbed of theirs. My father was only 26 years old when he died. Not much older than we were now.

I couldn't push the idea of that tape out of my mind. Skeptical as I was of Stan Man Duboclet, the pusherman himself, the tape had become hopelessly real to me. More real than Derrick or his crappy apartment or the dead fish and garbage stench or the sounds of the city or the footsteps on the other side of the ceiling. I stood there looking around the place, as if I might find that tape right there.

Chapter Three:

Darn that Dream

I found Derrick's MG parked around the corner near Avenue C and plucked three parking tickets off the windshield. His ignition didn't start right away and his clutch tried to give me a hard time, but I wasn't having it. In ten minutes I had that 5-speed Midget in the Holland Tunnel, then I-95 to Exit 70a, East Degraw, right on Teaneck Road, left on Cranford, and made the right turn into my mother's driveway a few minutes before ten o'clock. She had gotten there just ahead of me. Mom takes care of her Uncle Henry a few times a week, splitting the duties with two cousins. Uncle Henry was the pastor of our church until he got a brain tumor a few years ago. Now, he watches a lot of game shows and has to get fed his meals.

The front door of my mother's house was still open and inside my mother was lugging a bag of leftover food toward the kitchen. My hello startled her but she quickly found her breath and, without asking if I was hungry, fixed me a plate of chicken with rice and a bowl of pea soup. I didn't tell her why I'd come. Not right away. I kept it casual, which was not easy at that late hour. We tore off pieces from a long French bread and she gave me some gossip about the children of her friends. Gina Lamotte was having a baby. She had married a local police detective, a white man with children from a previous wife. Wilford Tinsley had dropped out of the community college but was supposedly making all kinds of money installing strobe lights in discothèques.

I pretended to be interested and every so often added an *mm-hm* or an *uh-huh*. Then I excused myself to the bathroom and snuck into the garage. I closed the door and turned on the light and looked around for a radio—something that could pick up WRVR Newark's late night tracks—but the only radio I found was AM and had no batteries anyway. An old refrigerator held a bottle of flat root beer. I didn't suppose there was much chance I was about to open a few boxes and find a tape no one had ever spoken about.

Being there brought back memories of looking for my father in that garage. I had spent a lot of hours doing that. Started when I was around ten years old. Till then I had tried to forget about the whole father thing. Mom was into forgetting, too. We'd become very close, did almost everything together and Mom kept things light. I had friends but they were mostly just to keep me from being alone at school. At home, where I spent most of my free time, Mom was enough. Then I got to having these dreams. In the dreams I was sitting on a piano bench, on my father's lap, watching his hands dance across the octaves, gasping for air in a haze of cigarette smoke, listening to that bebop. In the dreams I could only hear fragments, but it was still wonderful, the syncopated soul, and my father's caramel hands—the right one with that splotch of deep red—moving over those black and white keys and me trying to guess where they were going next.

I had that dream more than once so that in my memory I believed that there were many nights like that, but when I asked my mother about it—if it was real, if it was a memory or just a dream—she told me it was just one night. She said it was Minton's but I don't know whether to rely on her memory. For all I know that creep Duboclet had it right and it really *was* The Last Door.

One rainy Saturday, when I was about thirteen, I found my father's records in a crate in the garage. The Lonnie Baylor

Quintet with Felton Payne, Billy Heron, Cole Anderson, and Red Young. I listened to it for hours. My favorite cover was the one for *Struttin' with the LB 5.* It showed five pairs of feet in motion on a New York sidewalk, kicking up autumn leaves. I stared at that cover for the longest time trying to figure out which feet belonged to my dad. Probably the record label just found five guys with clean shoes and had them pose. I plugged in his old phonograph and I listened, and the magic came back to me. I closed my eyes, and I saw his hands, I smelled that smoke and the mixture of his aftershave and the butterscotch on his breath and I watched his hands caress the two-tone ivory.

Feeling that memory now, years later, had me remembering things I'd never remembered before: the way he'd return from a long trip, filling the doorway with his overcoat and his beret, one suitcase under each arm. He'd drop them and grab me. Always had something new and exotic to put in my hands, all the different bus tokens and post cards and key chains and music boxes and dolls from Chi-town and Motor City, Cinci and D.C. and Philly. My room was always full of all that stuff but I had made myself forget who it had all come from. I set up his old hi-fi in my bedroom, and for a long time after that would come home from school every day and lift the stylus arm and drop the diamond on a vinyl groove and transport myself. I don't think Mom dug what I was doing but what could she say? I'd lay across the floor and read liner notes and study the name of each cut and whose name was beneath the title in parentheses. My father's name beneath *Morningside Drive* had me believing it was the place where he had gone, that it was heaven. I used to imagine a warm Sunday afternoon kind of place with a light breeze and birds in formation, sun glowing, and my dad on a hillside with a mighty pearl-colored piano resonating across the sky. If I could only get there, I believed back then, he would see me and smile and I would touch his face and climb onto his lap and watch those hands. One afternoon I got hold of some maps in my junior high school library and found a Morningside Drive in Paterson and some weeks later I got Aunty Lorraine to drive me there. Needless to say, I didn't find my father or anyone else I knew or had ever known. Just a butcher shop and some public housing. A while later I found another Morningside Drive in Newark and took a bus down there and found a row of adult book stores. That summer I met an older cousin who still lived in New York City and she told me that the Morningside Drive my dad wrote about must have been the one in upper Manhattan. I got her to drive me across the bridge and down the Westside Highway and into Harlem. A lot of things came back to me when I traveled through the neighborhood where we had once lived, and Morningside Drive was a beautiful place, a place that fit that little chromatic letter, that lovely melody, Dad wrote—but of course he wasn't there, and by then I think I understood that the only place I ever would find him was in the music.

Morningside Drive was the first tune I ever learned to play, the first one I ever stumbled through a solo on. I took trumpet lessons at a place in Fort Lee, but Billy Heron was my real teacher, he and Lonnie Baylor. I'd listen to LB blow with Daddy on piano and then I'd play along. When I got a little older I had a friend whose father was a sound engineer at a local radio station and she got him to make me a recording of that cut without the horns so that it was just Dad and me and Cole Anderson on bass and Red Young on drums.

But my excavation of Daddy's things had never gone beyond the crates of records and the box that had housed his record player. Once I discovered the music, the rest of his stuff had seemed lifeless and sad.

Even now, as I hunched around that dusty garage, it all still got to me. I couldn't believe my mother never got rid of Daddy's old white shirts, his two ties—black with gold dots, gold with stars—his wool knit slacks, penny loafers and oxblood polish, the old shaving brush, mug and razor, the half-finished books of crossword puzzles and word jumbles.

I could hear my mother yelling for me in the house. I yelled back. Confessed where I was. She groaned from wherever she was, came to the garage door, and opened it, but didn't say anything. I kept digging—a box of letters and a few newspaper clippings someone must have stuffed in there. They were about the accident. Another shoebox contained sympathy cards I didn't read. A box slightly bigger than a shoebox had pennies and nickels scattered at the bottom along with a smashed watch, stuck forever on 2:12, and scraps of paper.

The paper scraps were pretty badly faded. Phone numbers without cities or area codes, some without names, next to phrases that were like the titles of songs never written: *Bossa For House Party, Baltimore Afternoon, Passing Glance, Didi's Mood*. I almost didn't notice one tiny, yellow crumple. It looked as though it might have been used to dispose of a piece of chewing gum. But it opened right up with a mist of twenty year old dust that threw me into a sneezing fit. I pressed it to the wall and flattened it enough to read.

> Things to do in Philly:
> *Call home*
> *Find laundry*
> *Buy Didi doll*
> *Listen to tape of tonight*

I read it twice, then again. I put that box down and dug deeper. Soon the dust became unbearable and I stumbled outside for fresh air. But immediately I thought about the possibility that that tape was right there inside that garage, just a few feet away, and had to go back inside.

But there was no tape. Not on any shelf or in any drawer or box.

I think Mom had forgotten about me because when I came back into the kitchen and let out one last big sneeze, she screamed, "Didi, you scared me!"

I told her what I had been looking for, and she said: "Didi, why do you do these things?"

"Because it's Dad playing like he'd never played before!"

"Let him rest."

Do you remember a box, about this big? Square, half an inch thick?"

She shook her head.

"Think back. Maybe the police in Delaware gave it to you."

"Uncle Henry picked up all the personal items and brought them here."

"Uncle Henry, you think he might have wound up with it?"

Mom just stood there, her eyes pleading with me. "You leave Uncle Henry out of this. The man has enough troubles." Then she smiled. "I guess I should be happy that you still think of Billy. I guess I should be proud."

"Do you still think of him?" I asked.

"I do. But it's hard, Didi. Maybe if I'd married again it would have been easier. Maybe not. I don't know. He'll always be a young man, and in a way that's good because when I remember him I remember being young too, but in a way it's bad, because he never grew up."

"But he did grow up, Mom, that's what I'm telling you. His last night, he stopped playing like a shy kid and took over the piano. "

Mom threw me a sideways glance. I hoped she wouldn't ask me where I got this information. She told me it was late, gave me new sheets for my old bed, and told me that when I woke up we would go over to Uncle Henry's and I could go through his cellar.

We got out early the next morning but hit some commuter traffic on the way over. I drove Mom's Buick and we talked about things. I let her know about Derrick and she showed her disappointment. Uncle Henry was happy to see us. He got all teary-eyed when I hugged him and he pulled my cheek against his. Mom kept him company and fixed oatmeal and coffee while I went down the cellar stairs. Uncle Henry had things pretty well organized, and it wasn't long before I figured out that tape was not in his possession. I was glad it was still early when we got back to Teaneck. I found a can of

Schlitz in my mother's refrigerator and drank half of it before I began gently pulling the crumbling news clippings out of the Hush Puppies box, reading them. Half a Schlitz wasn't nearly enough:

"The car was cut in half and the half Lonnie sat in was crushed, compressed like one of his unyielding high C-sharps," wrote some heartless scribe in a publication called Jazz Scene. "Pianist Billy Heron went through the windshield and lived long enough to mumble something about a flat tire. The woman, Shirley Townsend, was found twisted around the front axle. Reactions from around the jazz world: shock and horror at the deaths, but mostly at the loss of another young genius. 'First Bird, then LB,' said saxophonist, Felton Payne, who had played with Lonnie that night in Baltimore and was due to meet back up with Lonnie in Philadelphia for a date at The Black Eye. 'Just doesn't seem right. Lonnie shoulda outlived us all.'"

Chapter Four:

That Six-Four Feeling

I finished the beer and found the only album of the quintet in my mother's house (I guess I'd bogarted all the rest), an Emarcy anthology that had come out a few years ago. The first tune on the first side was Gershwin's *'S Wonderful* with that 6/4 feeling, the jazz waltz, and hearing my father's bright restrained chords I tried to imagine him letting loose in the way that Stan Duboclet had described, but I could hardly fathom it. This was LB's band, playing that Lonnie Baylor sound: hard-driving harmonies, a half-ironic you-better-love-life-or-you're-a-damn-fool sound. Not like Miles, trying to tear your heart to pieces, but Lonnie's lust, his spectacular technique, the wise phrasing; if you listen carefully, Lonnie could make this incomprehensible world fit together and show you that joy and pain are the same statement with slightly different punctuation. That LB sound—hearing it now made me believe that, yeah, if Billy Heron did step out that night at The Sound Box then there must be a tape of it and it could be found.

I sat back down and read another article, and then another. No mention anywhere of a tape surviving the crash. I took a nap on the couch in my mother's den and when I woke up she was gone. Probably back over at Uncle Henry's to make him lunch or just keep him company. I picked up the phone and got the area code for Glasgow, Delaware, and then the number of the Glasgow Police Department. The cat who answered seemed suspicious when I told him I needed information about a car accident twenty years ago. He put me on hold and then handed me over to someone else, a young voice about as helpful as anyone probably could have been. Wrote my number down and called me back an hour later after he'd located the police report of the accident. He agreed to read it to me over the phone:

"At two seventeen a.m. on February Twenty-seventh, Nineteen-Hundred and Fifty-Six a car carrying two Negro boys..."

"Who?"

"Haven't gotten to the names yet."

"They were not boys."

"Sorry, ma'am. I'm just reading what it says."

"Change it."

"Ma'am. This is a police report from twenty years ago and I'm an intern from the community college."

"Okay. I hear you."

"Here go their names. Lemont Calvin Baylor is one, and, William Lloyd Heron was the other. Want me to keep reading?"

"Can you send it to me?"

"I think so."

Three days later, I found the package from Glasgow PD sticking out of the mangled aluminum mailbox in the lobby of my building. I carried it upstairs where my roommate Carmen was asleep on the floor with headphones clamped to her head. I pulled photographs from the envelope but wasn't ready to look at them. I took them up to the roof of my building along with a tiny bottle of rum I'd found in Derrick's cupboard when I returned his car.

I sat on the building's ledge, overlooking narrow streets and the jigsaw puzzle of lower rooftops, and looked at the photos. The front half of the car appeared to have been chewed and spat. The rear was compressed to the size of a toboggan. Shredded suitcases dotted the clean snow. Blood-soaked glass splinters clung to trees. I tried to read the official report, skimmed over LB's "multiple head contusion," then the woman, Shirley Townsend's "lacerations and fractures," then I saw the name William Lloyd Heron and downed that rum while I read about his convulsions and the failed attempts to revive him. I kept on reading, looking for some mention of property recovered at the scene of the accident. The report mentioned a damaged trumpet found in the back seat and later given to "next of kin: deceased's mother, Dorothy Baylor of Washington D.C." It also mentioned "other various personal belongings given to above and to other next of kin: Mrs. William Lloyd Heron of New York City and brother of Shirley Townsend, Mr. A.C. Townsend, of Rochester, New York."

It took most of the following week to track down the whereabouts of Dorothy Baylor—Woodlawn Cemetery, died 1969 of lung cancer—and another two days to locate her only other child, daughter Silvia Baylor-Hernandez residing in Tampa. Silvia was pretty cool about my out-of-the-blue phone call. She seemed excited to hear from someone in connection with her brother, but then she confessed: "I didn't really know Lonnie very well. I was five years old when he left home and twelve when he died."

I told her I understood, that I was about the same age the last time I saw my father. She said it was great that I still cared about my father's music and she would do anything she could to help me, but when I asked her about the tape there was a long pause.

"Mom had his records," she said. "A few seventy-eights and a lot of LPs, but no tapes."

"Are you sure?"

"I remember pretty well. Lots of photographs, too, but not tapes. I gave everything to the Harlem Jazz Museum."

The next day after work I went to the 42nd Street Library and found a jazz encyclopedia that told me The Sound Box in Wilmington had burned to the ground in 1971. LB Quintet Bassist Cole Anderson was stabbed to death in 1966 by his manager. Felton Payne, according to the same source, died of a drug overdose in 1970. That left stick man, Red Young, as the only surviving member of the quintet. The encyclopedia said that he was "born Nelson Joshua Young in East St. Louis in 1925, studied clarinet at the Marshall Music Academy in Chicago, got his professional debut under the name Josh Young as a clarinetist with the WLLO radio dance orchestra in Cleveland in 1939. Returned from World War II in 1943 with shrapnel in his leg and turned up as a drummer for various dance and jazz big bands in Chicago and Milwaukee, then began periodically appearing with various short-lived combos on 52nd Street in New York City. In 1946, under the name Red Young, toured the Atlantic coast with Tadd Dameron's quartet, filled in with Charlie Parker and others. Recorded with Dizzy Gillespie and others. Four years keeping time in the Lonnie Baylor quintet, then left the jazz scene in 1956, one month after tragic Baylor car accident. Current whereabouts unknown."

I looked through the Downbeat Magazine archives and couldn't find anything else about Red Young, but did come across an obituary for Cole Anderson, the Lonnie Baylor Quintet bassist whose manager had taken a cut of more than just his earnings. Anderson left a widow named Cookie Anderson. I found someone by that name in the Manhattan White Pages. It took me about a week to reach the woman at home. I was in the bathroom. I'd pulled the long phone cord in there and closed the door to keep out the loud vocal exercises of an aspiring soul singer named Champagne, who was subletting Laquarie's corner of the apartment for the month.

I heard a faint hello on the other end of the line, told her I was Billy Heron's daughter, and asked if she was Cole Anderson's widow.

"What do you want?" she asked, and I told her why I was calling.

After a long pause she asked if I was from "the record company."

"What record company?" I asked.

"Don't play stupid with me, young lady. It's my tape." She cleared her throat and then seemed to have a conversation with someone who was there with her. I sat there waiting. "You want to buy that tape, don't you? Want to get your price. Well, it's my tape. My selling price. Don't you try to rip me off."

"You have the tape? The Sound Box? Nineteen Fifty-Six?"

"It's mine."

"How much do you want for it?"

"What record company you with?"

"I'm not."

"Don't lie to me. I'm *getting* my price. I want ten-thousand and a check every six months for what it sell. I'm not *going* to be ripped off like Cole let them, talking 'bout he want his money up front and come to find out they still sellin' records of him and we don't see nothin'."

"Ten thousand," I repeated. "Let me run that by my boss."

"See! I knew you's with a record company."

I felt bad lying to the woman—and a little scared. I wondered if impersonating a record-company executive was a felony? I still had the number I'd heard Nils Tanner leaving on Derrick's answering machine, on a scrap of paper in my purse. Called it. Took a while to get him on the phone but I was patient. I sat on the floor of the apartment with a pad of paper trying to write down what I would say to this guy and how to say it. Nothing looked right on the paper and I almost hung up when I heard his voice come on.

I told Nils Tanner who I was and reminded him that we'd met at Benet's a little while back.

"Yes," he finally said, "I remember. Your pianist owes me a call."

"He owes me a lot more."

Nils laughed—at least I think it was a laugh. He said, "So what can I do for you?" And I told him about the tape. That got him interested. "Have you listened to it?" he asked.

"She won't play it for me. She wants ten thousand dollars."

Nils laughed.

"Maybe she'll take less."

He put me on hold for a while and I waited there on the floor looking at all the crap my roommates and I had let accumulate beneath the long sofa.

Nils came back on the phone. "I'm willing to meet with this Cookie Anderson and see what she has, but I'm not quoting figures until I hear the tape and can make sure there are no other claims of ownership on it. What's her number?"

I flipped open the spiral tablet I'd been doing my research on and looked for Cookie Anderson's phone number. Then it hit me: "Wait. No. I want to be there."

"Do you have an interest in the tape?"

"Yes."

"I mean a business interest. Are you looking for a finder's fee because—"

"My interest is in hearing it. And other people hearing it. *You* hearing it. I want to be there."

He paused again and then gave me the address of an office on 7th Avenue near 55th Street and told me to tell Cookie Anderson to bring her tape there the next day at 2:00. I passed on the message and the Alamode address and offered to meet Cookie wherever she lived and travel together to the office, but she told me she wasn't interested in doing anything like that. She said she knew where to find 7th Avenue downtown.

Next morning I turned down a day's work at Jackie Robinson Junior High in East Harlem and did a little cleaning up around the apartment—since no one else ever seemed interested in doing any—and then walked down Broadway to 7th Avenue to a building above an electronics shop that was having a closeout sale on color organs. I knew so little about the business of records that I was unaware Alamode was the jazz label of a large conglomerate. I found that out after I tried to locate Alamode on the building directory, saw that they were on the top floor, and then walked out of the elevator to find big gold letters, embossed on a marble wall, spelling out The GLX Family of Labels.

By then the building AC had frozen a thin layer of perspiration against my skin. A long tinted window to my right looked down onto midtown, past the big white telephone company building and out to the Hudson and a wedge of the Jersey cliffs. On the wall across from all that was a collage, portraits of rock groups and pop groups and jazz legends all hanging out together and harmonizing in silence while classical music dribbled out of speakers tucked between the ceiling tiles. I announced myself to a receptionist who was too polite to be for real. She showed me where to sit. I found a Time Magazine and read about all the people trying to bogart their share of the Howard Hughes estate. An older lady in church clothes came out of the elevator a little while later, clutching a big handbag. With her was a big dude all pimped out in a maxi-suit and brim hat. He rolled a toothpick between his white and gold teeth. She told the receptionist she was Cookie Anderson and soon enough we were walking down a hallway lined with framed gold and platinum LP's that caught the ugly florescent light and turned it into metallic rainbows. We ended up in an office where Nils was waiting along with a younger cat— might have been his assistant, might just as likely have been his boss. They both wore jeans and T-shirts and talked to each other like there wasn't enough air in the room. Nils puffed a pipe with sweet smelling tobacco and sat in a vinyl chair with aluminum arms at a battered wooden desk piled high with papers, books, 8-track and reel-to-reel tapes. Behind his head a wall of framed photos—Nils with Dizzy and Roy Eldrige, Nat Cole, Stevie Wonder, Tito Puente, Thelonius Monk, Ella Fitzgerald, and Mercer Ellington.

Nils and his associate, who he introduced as Tyler, tried to keep it friendly but Cookie wasn't having it. She was a tired-looking woman with long curls coming across her face and down her cheek like black tears. She told Nils Tanner that her cousin, Edmond, was carrying a gun and wasn't afraid to go back to jail if they tried to swindle her out of the tape. Nils and Tyler looked at each other for a moment, then looked at me. I shrugged my shoulders. What did they want me to do about it?

"I want ten thousand dollars for this tape," Cookie Anderson said, and Tyler's reaction said it probably wasn't worth anything close to that. Nils said he'd have to hear it before they could discuss price. He reached out his hand for the tape and for a moment it seemed like Cookie Anderson wasn't going to give it to him. She looked at her cousin like he was supposed to just shoot everyone. He gestured to her to let go of the box.

"How do I know you aren't going to tape record it while it's playing and steal it from me?"

"We can't do that," Nils told her. "That tape is yours. It's the original."

"You're lying," she said, but then a secretary came in with a plate of crackers and cheese and some soda and juice, and that, more than Tanner's assurances, seemed to convince her to release the box.

Nils handed it to Tyler who took it to an electronic console on the far wall and threaded it up. He turned the play knob and we waited. First nothing, everyone looking at the floor. Then a long hiss, then a bass line.

Mrs. Anderson pressed a handkerchief against her left eye as she heard her late husband walking his instrument. I was all choked up too, anticipating my father coming in on piano.

But that wasn't what we heard.

The only other instrument was a saxophone. No piano—no drums or trumpet either. Just a duet, potent stuff but it was difficult for me to appreciate it through my disappointment. I thought they would fast-forward or stop it, but no one touched anything. Then Nils left the room and came back in with another man, this guy in a three-piece suit, and a woman with stringy hair tied up over her head and holding a small dog. They listened intently—even the little dog. Then Nils spoke over the frenetic bass and the whaling tenor: "We'll give you fifteen thousand."

Cookie Anderson asked for twenty and Nils, without hesitating, said yes. That was when I listened to the saxophone, really listened. It was John Coltrane.

The woman with stringy hair and the dog asked Cookie where the recording was made. She wasn't sure, but remembered John coming to their house in Stuyvesant Heights for a barbecue and the two of them playing while the food was on the grill. "Trane and Cole: the Barbecue Sessions," Tyler suggested. The man in the suit had another idea—which everyone pretended to like—call it: "Cookin' and 'Cuin."

Nils asked if Cookie or her cousin needed anything else to drink. He opened a liquor cabinet behind his desk and Edmond asked for Chivas Regal straight up. No one offered me anything, though Nils kept looking over, probably so he could find the right moment to politely show me the door. Eventually, he found it. He stood up and said, "Well, Didi, we don't want to take up any more of your time."

I didn't fight it. I got up and he was polite enough to walk me toward the elevator.

"I'll remind Derrick to give you a call," I said.

"Derrick? Oh, right, your pianist. Too late for the gig I had in mind but I'm always in need of a pianist with a strong left hand." He stuck out his right hand. "I'm sorry this didn't work out for you."

"Are you?"

He was thrown by my sudden bitterness. So was I.

We were near the end of a long hallway of framed album covers. Nils turned his body toward mine. One foot tapped the carpet. "What would you like me to do about it?" he asked.

"Help me find the tape. The tape of my father's last recording."

"How do you know for sure there even is a tape?"

I had the piece of paper I'd found in my mother's garage, my father's last to-do list and showed Nils where it said "listen to tape of tonight."

"You think I know where that tape might be?"

"I'll do the looking," I said. "I just need a little back up."

"You want me to pay you?"

"I'm just asking, sir. If you can just peel off twenty-G's for two guys farting around at a barbecue."

He held up a hand, not unkindly. "One of those guys is arguably the greatest—and undoubtedly the most popular—tenor players in the history of jazz. Real jazz, you know? And you know what? I still probably won't make back the investment. I just overpaid that woman for that tape. Probably by three-hundred percent. Know why? 'Cause it's nearly ten years since the man died and that might be the last piece of Trane anyone finds and I want it. Just like I overpaid for the *Bill Evans/Cannonball Adderley Garage Sessions* and for Louis Armstrong improvising on the deck of a Caribbean cruise ship. But between you and me, kid, jazz music is a losing proposition these days. The audience is dying, at least here in The States. It's a refined taste. Alamode is a tax write-off for the parent corporation. It's charity work, a public relations operation."

"Nothing wrong with that," I said. "So if it's a losing proposition anyway, why not throw me a few chips?"

He smiled. "I don't think so."

"I don't need a lot of money. Just a few thousand to pay my rent while I look for the tape and maybe a gun in case I have to deal with any other crazy-ass people like Cookie Anderson."

He laughed, and shook his head.

"Maybe I'll just go to another label. Maybe Blue Note or Verve want this tape more than you do!"

"Maybe," he said, and turned to walk away.

"Fuck you," I said, and he turned back.

Losing it like that was the last thing I wanted to do—but I had done it. Nothing left to do now but let it all out on the guy. I froze him with my anger. Other people in that hallway found an excuse to duck around the corner or into an office. It was just me and Nils. "Yeah, you don't owe me. Don't owe me a damn thing. Nothing in any contract says you've got to even give me the time to say what I've got to say. But what about all them?" I pointed up at all the gold and platinum records and at the artists on the jackets of those albums. "You didn't owe them much either, did you? Still don't. You worked that out, didn't you? How many copies have you sold? How many are you still selling, after ten years? After twenty years—thirty years? How much of it did they get? They put their souls on your vinyl and half of them gonna die broke. 'Cause you don't owe anybody."

I had him. I knew it and so did he. Nils didn't say anything. Wouldn't look at me either. But he stood there. Trapped. I don't even know if half of what I said was right. Didn't matter. There was enough truth to pin him to the wall right below the album jacket of *Dexter Gordon at Montreux*. Without the music there is no record label, no parent company. But that wasn't even it. Without the music, there's nothing but dull conversation and a two-drink minimum, no sound to help the soul heal or the mind remember. So, yeah, Nils Tanner had a debt. Him and everyone else in that office. A debt to every player who ever laid down a track anywhere under any circumstances. Like Long Tall Dex, up there on the wall. LTD never held anything back. He left it *all* there on that stage in Montreaux—like my father who held nothing back that last night, my father who left it all, his blood and hope and memories on the clean snow of that dark road.

Chapter Five:

The Heartbeat

Nils gave me three months and $3000 and I don't think he expected me to find anything. No reason he should have. I had no idea what I was doing. Like a player without range or style, without a true sound trying to work it out on a long solo—as if inspiration could invent some chops.

I called my Local, Musician's Union 802, on a hot morning with rain beating against the windows, thunder ringing out from across the river. I asked the guy on the other end of the line about LB's tenor man, Felton Payne, and the guy asked me who I was. Of course, first he told me I was late with my own membership dues. I promised to mail a check that afternoon. Then he let me know that Felton Payne had stopped paying his dues in 1966. Said someone named Y. Beasly in Scranton, Pennsylvania, had produced a death certificate for him in 1972 and was now being sent the royalties, such as they were: about $112 a year. I tried to find Y. Beasly but directory assistance in Scranton had no listing. I was about to catch a train down there but when I called Local 802 back to double check it, the voice of an older woman, tired and impatient, told me that for two years everything they'd sent there had returned with no forwarding address. She asked if I wanted to make a claim to those royalties.

The rain outside had stopped and the streets below still glistened in the soft wind. Droplets on the window panes slid sideways. I asked the impatient lady about Lonnie Baylor's dummer, Red Young. Turned out his royalties were so small the union was no longer obliged to send them.

Back at the library, I spent a long afternoon in a room full of telephone books from around the world and wrote down the area codes and numbers of everyone named Red Young, R. Young, Joshua Young, J. Young, J.N. Young, and J. Nelson Young. I checked greater New York, Chicago, Philadelphia, Los Angeles, San Francisco, Kansas City, Miami, Orlando, Houston, Dallas, and Detroit. I filled three yellow legal pads, then went home and pulled the phone and a bag of Chips Ahoy into bed with me and started dialing, asking over and over: "Are you Red Young the drummer?"

The answer was always the same.

I must have called one hundred or more and then fell asleep. I woke up and climbed scales on my horn until someone a few floors down yelled that his baby couldn't sleep. It was a humid night, still early. I rode the IND uptown to that building with the rooftop jam sessions in Washington Heights. The elevator never came so it was twelve flights up. The roof was empty. I looked out over the northern stretch of the island beneath iridescent clouds and heard the distant thunder that had encircled the city all day and thought it had intimidated my musical friends. But then I saw them, about four blocks away, the rooftop Afro-Cuban jazz party. I went down to the street and tried to find the right building. The sidewalks were piled with bags of rotting garbage. The smells and all the looking up and looking down got me dizzy until I nearly said forget it. But then I caught the red glow of a cigarette butt, plummeting in front of me like a dying firefly. I glanced up and saw a human butt hanging off a ledge, a drink cup spilling over and then suddenly I could feel the pulse of the music. I went up there, licking my chops for some harmonizing. I stepped out onto the roof, showed the dude at the door my horn so he didn't try to take my money, and then looked out at the funky little band-stand. It was overrun with congu-eros and horn players. Six trumpets and a bunch of saxophones. I found a spot at the edge of the music and added what I could and tried to feel a part of it but I could swear no one noticed me. I didn't mind it, not really. The energy of the music was passing through me and I was kissing the hot sound through my brass valves. But after a while I felt tired and my ears hurt and my jaw got all tense so I lowered my horn and walked out as unnoticed as I'd walked in—except for one dude in a Boricua cap who told me he liked the way my jeans fit. On the subway back downtown I did something I'd never done. I took out my instrument and played into the deafening roar between stations. I played Monk's *Bemsha Swing* and Mobley's *Syrup and Biscuits*. I missed my stop and ended up down in Times Square. I played in the station for a while until a cat with an alto and a peddle drum came up and told me it was his spot. I told him no problem and did a little harmonizing to his *Lush Life*. I went up to the street and wandered around, hauling that horn and thinking about every player who ever walked 7th Avenue and 8th Avenue and tried to make a life of sound work out, get enough folks to listen and try to be all right with it when folks didn't listen. I went into a Sam Goody record store and looked around with no intention of buying and did something I hadn't done since I was about 15 years old. I flipped through the H's—Chico Hamilton, Herbie Hancock, John Handy, Barry Harris, Eddie Harris, Eddie Henderson, Joe Henderson—to see where I might one day fit: between John Hendrix and Gil Scott-Heron (no relation to me, that I know of). I wondered why they put Gil in jazz. I guess they didn't know where to put him and I guess, really, no one knows what jazz is anymore or what any musical categories ought to be. I left the H's and turned and wandered the aisle, looking at the few other lost souls looking for jazz near 11 o'clock on a spring night in the middle of the week. I looked in the P's. Felton Payne had his own section with four reissues and an anthology called *The Felton Payne Memorial Album*. I looked in the Y's and found Lester Young and Webster Young and Larry Young but nothing by Red Young. I went back to the B's, pulled the Lonnie Baylor tab, as if the tape might have been filed there, by God. I heard a voice behind my head and jumped. The security guard told me it was closing time. I eased toward the front door and had to wait for the guard to drag his ass over and unlock it. He asked me if I was hungry and I almost said yes, because I was, suddenly, starving, but I caught myself and didn't say anything and he didn't bother me while I lingered in the doorway, looking at all the flyers and posters: apartments to share and used instruments for sale and live jazz in the city. I saw Derrick's name. He had a quartet playing at a club downtown called The Fish Tank.

I went down there and caught the second half of the last set. I paid the cover but dodged the waitresses and didn't buy any drinks. The place was cramped and stuffy with mildew and perfume but Derrick and his guys were making everyone forget about all that. I don't know who they were. Not his bass or his drums or the half-black, Chinese-looking dude who got up and played alto on one tune or the chick who got up and sang *You Go To My Head*. Derrick was working those keys and had all the players gently massaging the air with him, phrasing it fresh, making those soft impressions, holding up the beauty of the music without letting the familiar get obvious. The music just wrapped its arms around me and had me spinning in a good state until it was over and I got hit with the betrayal of it all. D saw me before I could slip away and saw that I was carrying my trumpet case.

"Didi. You should have said something. I didn't know you were here."

"Yeah. I almost didn't know you were here either."

"Right," he said, nodded, his head sinking, face all crunched so that I was supposed to think he was ashamed. "I'm not supposed to see you."

"You're not supposed to see me?" I guess my voice was a little loud. Derrick pulled me through a side door, into an alley. He looked over his shoulder at his bass player and if I'd seen Derrick's expression I probably would have punched him, but I didn't. I said, "*You* can't see *me*?"

"My sponsor from the Paragon House says no emotional attachments for my first year."

"I guess you're not emotionally attached to your music."

"Hey, you could have sat in. You should have let me know."

"I didn't come here to beg my way onto your band stand."

"Why *did* you come here?"

"I don't know," I said and turned to walk away, and nearly walked into a wall of garbage. If collective humanity has a butt crack that is what that alley smelled like. But at this point I was just about immune.

"Wait," Derrick said. "Let's talk. I do miss you."

I half-turned back. "Should I call your sponsor."

He laughed. "What's new, kid? Let's go for a walk. I'm done here."

"So am I. You can walk me to the subway."

He did. It was only a few blocks away. He asked me what I was up to and I told him nothing but he pressed me to talk and I didn't want to seem like I was hiding from anything. I told him about the tape and he got all excited and that made me want to get out my horn and duet with him again, one more time. But I kept that to myself. Told him how I was getting nowhere in my search and he said, in his usual state-the-obvious-like-a-revelation way, "Why don't you find Red Young? The drummer. Maybe he's got it."

"Thanks for the advice, Derrick, but I don't know where to find Red Young."

"Try Disneyland," Derrick said and I laughed, because I thought it was a lame joke. "Why you laughing?" he asked.

"You sending me to the Magic Kingdom to find a missing reel of bebop?"

"I got an aunty in L.A., and my mom sent me there for the summer like six, eight years ago. It was right after I dropped out of high school the first time. She wanted me away from her so she put me on a Greyhound for five days...I ran out of food on the third. Aunty took me to Disneyland, which was actually the scariest place I had ever seen. Hardly any black people and white people lookin' crazy at me and everyone was like off the Brady Bunch but half of them angry enough to lay a brotha out. But I did trip off the Mississippi River Boat thing. Had a Dixieland band onboard. I thought I recognized the drummer but I couldn't figure out where. Then I went to a record store and browsed around until I came across the back of an album cover—one of those LB Quintet sides, I think—and it had a picture of Red Young. That was him. I know it was. Can you believe that shit? Dude played with Charlie Parker, was the heartbeat of the LB Five, then he drops out of the scene and winds up in a novelty band at Disneyland!"

A phone call to Disneyland confirmed it. Joshua Young had worked there sixteen years before retiring. Disney personnel wouldn't divulge his current whereabouts but when I asked for a supervisor she agreed to pass on a message. Two days later, I came in the apartment and dropped a bag of groceries to get to the phone which I'd heard ringing from a flight below. The faint voice on the other end of the phone said, "This is Red Young. I'm calling for Didi Heron." He pronounced it almost like Heroine. Sounded like he was calling from a factory.

I asked him where he was and he said, "I'm in the desert. Rancho Mirage. How you like that?" Then he asked me what record company I was from.

I told him Alamode and he told me to come see him at the Musician's Union Local, 47 Max Steiner Hall, and gave me an address on Victory Drive. Said he had something I'd definitely want to listen to.

I'd never been to Los Angeles and I was excited to be going. From the air, at night, L.A. looked like a giant radio thrown off the top of a mountain and shattered on a hard floor. It was almost ten o'clock by the time I threw my luggage into the trunk of a rented Dodge Dart and found the Airport Marriott. When I woke up the next morning I stretched out on the queen-sized bed and enjoyed some room service. I got a nice guy at the front desk to send up some maps so I could plot out the drive to Rancho Mirage. L.A. wasn't like the postcards. The air was light brown, and the mountains looked like shadows, but there was a 24-hour jazz station to keep me company on the Christopher Columbus Interstate 10 Freeway. KBCA was featuring musical selections in which the musicians talked at the beginning and/or end of the tune. "Listen out for Jimmy Heath asking for a bottle opener," said the DJ, Sam Fields, who then spun *J's Mood,* and at the end you could hear someone asking about something, but I couldn't make out a single word. Then a very nice version of *Soul Eyes* by someone on alto with guitar was followed by the garbled voice of a musician saying, "The plumber has arrived!" But soon I was leaving the L.A. basin and the signal was fading. The air lightened up and I could see some mountains sketched jaggedly into the clouded sky, could see miles of sand and cacti on either side of the road.

Rancho Mirage lived up to its name. The convenience stores and gas stations and condominiums didn't seem real against the harsh colors of the desert. Steiner Hall sat a few blocks from the highway, a long adobe palace in a sea of parking spaces.

I parked and got out. The heat had a thick rubber taste and the high voltage of cicadas made it feel even hotter. The front door was heavy and squeaked a B-flat. A statue of Max Steiner conducting an imaginary orchestra greeted me in the bright lobby along with the smell of rose water and mint deodorizer.

"You must be from the record company," someone said, a white-haired lady in a pink kimono, standing against an oddly placed Roman column. She had the kind of New York accent that sounds European. Her smile was a thick rope across her face. "This way, darling." She grabbed my elbow, said her name was Ruby Saffron and when I tensed my arm she looked fiercely at me. She told me she had been the singing voice of Rita Hayworth and Jane Mansfield in several of their films, then pulled me around a corner, past portraits of a man with a clarinet that might or might not have been Benny Goodman and into a large room that echoed with the eerie repetitions of what sounded like moisture discharging through a drainpipe.

"There he is," Ruby said, aiming her eyes at the far corner, where a lone figure swung a set of mallets at the bars of an old set of vibes. Ruby released her grip on me and I made my way toward the vibraphonist. I didn't get too close. I watched and waited. He was a slight man. His shirt and slacks hung around him like a flag. He had a band-aid on one cheek and a rash on his forehead. The sleepy eyelids and the crooked mouth I recognized from the cover of *Sublimity* and *I Go to Your Head* and other LB Five album covers. I couldn't believe I was in the presence of Red Young. He had been my drummer all these years while I played along with my father's records. Now here he was, an old man playing the vibes in creaky patterns. Soon he was joined by an even older-looking dude, a white guy with round black specs, dull gray hair looping across a liver-spotted dome, and a scuffed string bass and bow which he sawed away in queer harmony with Red's vibings. They seemed to be playing some kind of upside down permutation of *Stompin' at the Savoy*.

The smell of poached eggs and coffee hovered around us. People circled the doorway, staring in. The two old men stopped playing suddenly and turned toward me with vigorous anticipation. I wasn't sure what to say. All I could think of was, "I didn't know you played vibes."

"I play piano, clarinet, bassoon, and vibraphone."

"And drums," I added.

Red smiled, unfolded a cracked pair of glasses and stared at me through them. "You must be that woman from the record company. Which one?"

I told him and he lifted his head. "Meet Carlton Von Schmidt," he said, and the man with the double bass bowed. He stuck out a gnarled hand, tobacco stained, and I shook it.

"Know who he is?" Red Young asked. "Modern day reincarnation of Bartok, Beethoven, and Bach, man. Boy played with many many great orchestras in the world. New York. Chi-town. Texas. Played on the soundtrack of mucho great movies, too. TV shows."

Carlton stepped forward and announced, "I wrote *Theme from the Outlaw Trail*. The last five bars, they were mine—but they stole the credit."

"Boy taught me a whole lot," Red said, winking at Carlton, who gave me a sharp stare. "Music theory and all kind of very intricate niceties. And I taught him a little. And we got to thinkin one morning bout a new sound. Whole new breed of sound. Two dudes from Germany won a peace prize about the cells in a body talkin to each other. Am I right?" Red asked Carlton, who hummed agreement and put a Menthol 100 backward in his mouth. He held up the flame of a lighter, then at the last second, before igniting the filter, turned the cigarette around and lit it properly. "Little cells," Red went on. "Can't see nothin, tiny tiny, speakin the message in secret code to other tiny tiny. Secret code messages bout how we gonna live and die in this world and can't hardly hear none of it." He winked at me. "But if we could!"

Carlton's stomach gurgled and I thought for a moment that it was part of their musical composition, because right afterwards Red launched into a minor vamp on the vibes with Carlton flicking the long strings of his bass.

It certainly was a new sound, but I'm not sure you could say much more about it. I tried to seem interested. I did think it was cool that these two old cats weren't just stuck in their past. I applauded when it was over, and said, "That's really something."

"You damn right," Red said, setting down the mallets.

I told them I liked their new sound and they ought to keep on keeping on with it. It had possibilities. I was as full of shit as any real executive in the music industry. I told them they were on the right track, then waited for enough silence to make a smooth transition to: "Is the tape still available?"

"Our tape?" Red asked.

"The Lonnie Baylor tape," I said.

Carlton waved an accusatory finger at Red. "What's she talking about?"

"The last performance of the quintet," I said. "At The Sound Box in Baltimore. You said you had it."

Carlton said, "You're not here for our music, are you?"

Red's eyelids sank and a veiny hand pinched his forehead. Carlton's stomach was squealing like an angry pig. He puffed on his cigarette and blew a cloud of smoke in my face with the word, "Go." He held the incendiary tip of his cigarette out toward my eye. "You get out of here now, you philistine! You've nearly killed him." He followed me as I retreated toward the doorway. "Go on," he kept saying. "You just go on, young miss."

And I had every intention of doing just that. Drive the hell out of there, get back to New York. Forget the whole thing. But then I remembered those photos I'd seen of the accident and I thought, *Red Young and that other dude, they hadn't died that night in the snow. Didn't know a damn thing about pain.* I turned around, as if I might just say those exact words to their faces. Red was looking right at me, his face all crumpled. He waved at me, then mouthed the words:

"Come back. Please come back. Come back tomorrow."

I found a motel with a vacancy sign and got myself a room. It was crazy being out there. I wasn't exactly the only black person, but almost, and while I didn't feel anyone's hostility there seemed to be a lot of suspicion. When I went out to get dinner, one old fool in a Barracuda convertible took me for a hooker and tried to wave me over. I tried not to take it personally.

Back at the room I collapsed on the bed and thought about the music I'd heard at Steiner Hall. I wanted to dig the erratic instrumental of Red Young and his friend. Wanted to tell myself it was a sound that Mingus might make if he got together with Milt Jackson, reaching for the melodic shape of things to come. From Mingus and Bags it would be important music.

Next morning Red was waiting for me outside Steiner Hall in a small ragged garden. His slight figure was more defined in stiff jeans, a starched white shirt, a purple and orange ascot, and a teal cardigan. He wore a black porkpie hat, worked a wad of gum, and swatted at a fly as I pulled up in the car.

His right leg was dragging his left leg toward the passenger door, hips swinging in 4/4 time. He got in next to me. It was already hot as hell outside and the whine of the car AC made him have to raise his voice:

"Young lady, I am sorry for what happened yesterday."

"It was my fault. I should have been more clear about my purpose."

"Wasn't nobody's fault. And I'm sorry about my boy Carlton. Don't know why I put up with that fool. But he helped me after Helen passed away. You know, that's why I moved here, when she got sick with the cancer. We shared that room in hell together. I thought we would just die *together*—but I'm still here. There's this Mexican place." He pronounced it Meskin. He blew a gum bubble and grinned. His teeth were small and grainy. "You got enough gas in this car?"

I didn't want to seem pushy about the tape, so I kept the conversation loose while we drove. Gilbert's Cantina was busy feeding a squad of construction workers. Two men with the weary eyes of salesmen stood in line ahead of Red and me. Red kept almost leaning into me.

We reached the counter and ordered, then found a table. They were wooden picnic tables with plastic red and white checkered table cloths. The tacos were good but the hard shells broke in my mouth and splintered in my hands.

Red's eyes narrowed as he ate. He picked up a bottle of Tampico hot sauce and his mind seemed to drift. "Memory," he said, "is a sometime thing. My head gets light as the air and the door to yesterday just opens up. Faces and places and empty spaces. But it ain't what I want to remember. Like Helen. My wife. I don't hardly see her in them thoughts. Just things. Things I forgot even happened. Stuff didn't mean nothin to me at the time. An electrician in a cowboy cap tapin up a connection at The Horn Stable, y'understand, or Flip Phillips helpin me break down my kit in a studio in Hackensack."

"How's your memory for that last gig in Baltimore?" I asked, sipping beer from a styrofoam cup.

"That night was a monster, and a guy named..." Red grabbed his beer cup. "Guy named—what was his name? Old boy with the dope and the recording machine." Red took a long swig of foam.

"Stan Duboclet."

"Stan Man! You a smart girl. Smart smart. I know you know what that tape was all about. Lonnie, my man, was the main man of the young trumpet players on the scene, up and comin. I mean, there was a lot of up and comers at that moment. Lee Morgan, Clifford Brown, Miles Davis, Don Byrd, Joe Gordon. Rippin it up. But especially Lonnie Baylor." Red put a forkful of rice and beans in his mouth and picked up his beer again. His hand shook and he wet his chin. "I can still smell the burn of them lightening riffs so smoothly comin out Lonnie's horn. I was the heartbeat," Red said, stabbing his burrito. "I was the heartbeat, man. I close my eyes and I still see the way the spotlight made sparks fly off the sides of LB's horn every time he blew and with the smell of his inspiration perspiration. I was the heartbeat, man. Keepin time for genius. Genuis time." He took another forkful and asked, "Why you not eatin your stuff?"

"It's a lot of food," I said. He kept looking at my tacos and me not eating them and those sad old eyes had me grabbing up a broken piece, bringing it to my mouth.

Red slurped his beer with a faraway grin. "The Sound Box it was called. The club that night. Make me cry just to think about it." And as he said it I felt myself start to cry. I held it back, but my throat got dry and my nose started to run. "Changed the name after the wreck," he said. "That's what I heard. Birdland South. Course, now ain't no Birdland South or North. Was a hell of a night, though. One swingin affair." Red wiped his cheek with his hand, pulling the flesh taut, making a vein protrude and in it I could read the man's pulse. Slow and steady. The heartbeat still beating. His eyes glazed over and he seemed to meditate, then took three hefty rhythmic bites of his burrito and chewed with his click-clacking jaw. "Blizzard outside," he said, finally, "but inside was hot, hot, lava hot."

"What tunes did you play?"

Red stopped chewing. "That was about twenty years ago, my sweet. I do know how we ended the first set."

"How's that?"

"*Now's the Time*. You know the Bird had just died and we honored him toward the close of the first set—every time, pretty much. No, wait a minute. Wasn't the end of the first set. That was something else...Can't remember. But we did honor the Bird. Sometime. During the second set I do believe now. In the middle. Toward the end. Was a regular thing. Some nights we'd play *Moose the Mooch*, sometimes *Ornithology, Crazyology, Quasimodo, Drifting on a Reed*. This night it was *Now's The Time*. We tore it up. Felton led in, tenorizing sweet-strongly like, yeah, now *is* the time, baby! Five black men on the stand not backing down. This 1956, y'understand, wasn't no Civil Rights Amendment or none a that, but we had somethin to say about it, that night. Then Lonnie snuck up from behind, playin half a bar back of Felton, like a echo chamber, talkin bout *now's* the god-damn *time,* one way or the other. And I was slappin that snare between the two of them, exclamation points on the message. Cole's bass line was a warning from the underground, oh yeah!"

"What about Billy?"

"Billy?"

"On piano. Billy Heron."

"Yeah, he was there," Red said, nothing more.

"How did Billy play?" I asked, but Red didn't seem to hear. The next thing he said was:

"Man, and when we soloed, it was upstairs to God, let him know now *was* the time. Yeah, I'll have to have me a good look for that tape." He poured what was left of his beer into his mouth and sloshed it around, then swallowed and burped with high-pitched abandon. "I'm glad to be talkin about it," he said. "Shoulda done it twenty years ago. That tape, you know, it was the only thing made it, really. Somehow, when the car flipped, the tape musta flew out. Big old reel-to-reel box of tape. Landed on a snow drift they told me."

"Who told you?"

"Said they didn't understand how the tape got out the car. Car caught fire, you know. Windows musta broke just as the tape let fly. Found it twenty some feet away."

"And they just handed it to you?"

"We was in the motel next morning when we found out. Me and Felton. Road manager sent us a telegram. We went to Delaware. Policeman had their things."

"How does it sound?"

Red looked down at the speckled linoleum floor. "Ain't never heard it."

"Has anyone ever listened to it?"

"Don't know. Not to my knowledge."

"But you have it."

Red's shoulders tilted toward an uneven shrug. "Like I said, time to start lookin, and even better time to listen if I can just find it. I'm so happy that a young person still cares about the music. Make me wanna listen. Make me feel strong." He reached out and squeezed my hand. I felt his excitement and it gave me a chill. "Did I tell you how we opened the show?" he asked.

"Tell me," I said and squeezed back.

"Pretty thing, a ballad in high speed that made the audience bop and cry at the same time. Thing called *Morningside Drive*."

"Billy's tune. That must be what got him going that night."

"Billy *Heron*!" Red stabbed the last piece of his burrito. "Billy wasn't shit. Man, we shoulda had Hank Jones in that quintet. Or Mal Waldron, Sonny Clark, Kenny Drew. Man, Billy was a sad little punk, that's all. Stupid sorry ass gonna let that *woman* drive the car. Didn't nobody miss Billy."

I watched him say all these things, stared at his mouth like I couldn't make out the words, like they were just noises coming out of him. I noticed how bloodshot his eyes had gotten and how they seemed to have come closer together on his face. I don't think I'd ever heard a bad word about my father before or met anyone who disliked him. I had to check myself. Had to ask myself if I was all right. I pulled my hand away from his cold hand and hoped he would shut up, but he was speaking from a part of himself that seemed as inflamed as the part of me he was hurting. "We had rules in the band," he said, "but, oh, no, not for Billy Heron. Billy was a punk, man! He took LB away. Busted up our thing. Destroyed our friend. Twisted him up and his sweet horn. Put a part of me in that grave with him."

I had to excuse myself from the table and hurry to the ladies room in the back. It was tiny, clean—clean enough. I stood at the sink, trying to get my bearings. I had to remind myself, *You are Didi Heron. You are in a place called Rancho Mirage. But what just happened was real.* I didn't know whether to cry or punch the wall. It didn't seem fair for Red to say those things with my father unable to defend himself. And it didn't make sense. I guess in my mind Billy Heron was perfect.

Chapter Six:

Spontaneous Combustion

I must have stayed in that restroom a long time, staring at the walls, mostly counting time with my breathing. Someone knocked on the door and I told whoever it was to wait. Then I thought about what Red had just told me—before he'd started talking mess about my father. About *Now's the Time* with each player making his point. I started remembering all the times I'd thought *now's the goddamn time!* I imagined my dad at the piano telling the world that now was the goddamn time for him, and I decided that his musical truth of that night needed to be heard regardless of anything. I could see it and hear it in my mind and then something hit me that I felt to the marrow. I guess I'd never thought about it before, but seeing Red sitting there, a different man than he must have been twenty years ago, but a man nonetheless, made me think for the first time what a shame it was that Billy Heron never got to know that part of life. Or see jazz musicians getting their due. Or see me become a woman. Those were the thoughts that turned me around and sent me back through that door. Because there was only one way Billy Heron ever could be here in the present again and get the recognition he deserved.

"Everything all right," Red asked when I returned to the table.

"Yeah," I said, "everything is all right."

Then I took him home, told him we'd start looking tomorrow.

That afternoon, with my room's air conditioner rattling on high and that chemical cold air up in my nostrils, I telephoned Nils Tanner at Alamode Records and told him where I was.

"You got that tape?" he asked.

"Not yet," I said. Through the window, storm clouds rose up over the mountains. Seemed like that was an every day thing, a pending storm that would just pass over us toward some other mountains.

"What's the problem?" Nils asked.

"No problem. I just got here."

"Did you make contact with Mr. Young?"

"Yes."

"Does he have the tape?"

He was asking the same questions I'd been asking but from Nils they were annoying as hell, so I told him to calm down. "They played *Now's the Time,*" I told him. "Their tribute to Charlie Parker. Twenty-four hours later and cats all over the world were blowing tributes to Lonnie Baylor."

"Yeah," Nils said, deferentially.

"They played like men," I said. "They made *Now's the Time* into a political statement! Then it jumped out of the car like it had to, like it knew, like it was jumping to save its life." I imagined a flat square box gyrating around the inside of the car. "It was the middle of winter and the windows were rolled up. That tape bounces off the ceiling, off the seats. A window shatters and it flies just before the car burst into flames. Snow and ice everywhere, but the damn thing falls between the roots of an elm tree and stays dry. The *only* thing to survive. The only thing. Red Young wound up with it but the man couldn't bring himself to listen to it—never has. No one has ever heard it. Twenty years later, he's ready to share it. His own final gesture to the jazz world."

"I want that tape," Nils said. "Let me know if you need any more money. I'll be in L.A. next week. We got Natural Fact in studio. I'll call you when I get out there. God, I want that tape. Alamode presents: *Lonnie Baylor, One Last Time...* Rescued from the inferno, then from oblivion. *Lonnie's Last Jam*. Or maybe just the simple truth: *LB Lives*."

One wall of Red Young's room had a crooked poster of kittens in a drawer. The other had a shelf stacked sideways with a tattered set of encyclopedias, magazines, and coloring books, plus a photo of a small child throwing a kiss. Next to the shelf was a window with a wide sill piled high with sections of yellowed newspapers, tuna cans, and pieces of junk mail disguised as telegrams.

"I wish I had the heart to do this on my own. Can't even go through my own stuff. Got to have you here."

"Don't worry about it."

"Here I am maybe living with the tape. You'd think I'd open a drawer and have a look. Not so."

I reached for the top right desk drawer. It wouldn't budge.

"Lotta stuff in there," Red apologized, then showed surprising strength, dislodging the stuck drawer. It was packed with old check registers and personal date books, picnic napkins, a plastic rain hat, skin creams, pennies. The other drawers contained more of the same kind of rummage, as did the upper shelves of his closet. Then the shoe boxes under the bed. Photographs. Red bit his lip. His eyelids hung over his eyes as he stared down at one after another.

Red handed me a photo of the same little girl who was smiling on his wall. I admired the wild bushy hair, the black lashes and bluish eyes, a candy cane in one tiny hand, a stuffed

Cookie Monster in the other. "Man," Red said, "She ain't been by for a while."

"Your granddaughter?"

Red nodded his head. "Anya. Last visit, it tore me up. We picked flowers outside, then played piano together in the dining room. That child loves the piano. Loves to finger around on it with me. People used to come inside to hear us. I think she liked that. It was February. Rainin that day, so the piano was off key. Anya didn't care, so neither did I. Played her a uptempo *Twinkle Twinkle*. Anya got to bangin on keys, played like a set of wind chimes. I laid some sweet blues line 'neath her slammin jammin thing. Anya give me a big hug and said, 'Do that again.' I didn't know what she wanted me to repeat but I just smiled back and kept doing what come naturally. If I coulda froze time—*man*." He swung his head against one shoulder and shut his eyes. Then opened them and looked right at me. "I don't know where I woulda froze it. That night back in '56 at The Sound Box, or that afternoon here with Anya. Don't know."

I sat there listening and for a minute stopped caring about the tape. I imagined his granddaughter, his little girl on his lap playing piano with him and there wasn't anything else I wanted to do except to share that.

"The road, man," Red mumbled. He kept mumbling that same phrase. "The road, man. What it take from you, can't get it back. My boy, Lou, and his girl Anya. And LB and everything. The road is a mothafucka."

The next day, Red had me take him to a diner where other men he seemed to know grinned and winked from the counter when they saw that I was with him. Red ate an open-faced chiliburger and told me just how much he disliked the barber who came to the hall once a week and if it wasn't too much trouble we could stop at the place where Frank Sinatra always got his hair cut. Frank wasn't there—so I was the celebrity of the day, a "big record producer" working on a project with Red.

Down the block was a shoe repair that could (on the Alamode Records tab) resole the shoes Red had custom made for his narrow flat feet—on a quiet afternoon in Detroit twenty-three years ago—so that he could now walk around in comfort while he looked for the tape. At the other end of town, just a "quick" twenty-five minute drive, was a tobacco store that sold Dominican by the box. Those cigars had been the aroma of the backstages along 52nd Street in the late 1940's and early 1950's. Anything to help shake his memory.

It took most of a week to search Red's room. Every day a mixture of spontaneous errands to inspire recollection, interruptions from Carlton and his angry stomach and his acerbic tongue. Red had a ridiculous number of containers crammed into his ten-by-twelve room. Most of them he was surprised to discover. None contained a single reel of magnetic tape.

"I got to fix my mind," Red told me at the end of one of those endless afternoons, puffing cautiously on one of the Dominicans.

"Relax," I told him. "You'll remember."

"I'm tryin." He sniffed the sides of the burning cigar and mumbled, "Why did he get in that damn car. Man, even if he did lose his train ticket. He was a little too crazy, y'understand."

"You talking about Lonnie?"

"Course I am. He thought he'd live forever and everything work out. You got to understand, that was his mentality, what came out his horn. Said everything is everything and nothin is really that bad. Had a toothache one time. We was walkin the Harlem River Drive and the boy was just screamin at the night. Hadn't been to a dentist since he was twelve. I took him next day. Dentist must have worked on him all mornin long, and told Lonnie he couldn't play trumpet for a month. Lonnie said that was an impossibility. Dentist said at least then hold off for two weeks. Lonnie said fine. Problem was we had a date that afternoon with Prestige cross the river, y'understand. LB had done the arrangements with Felton; they was tough. We tried to postpone the date, but the producer said it couldn't be done. We tried everyone who was around that day—Carmell Jones, Blue Mitchell, Clifford Brown, everyone—tryin to replace Lonnie, but couldn't nobody get over there in time so we decided to go with a quartet. Billy would vamp in some of the trumpet charts and Felton would wail double time. We got in the studio. It was too cold in there 'cause the furnace was half-broke, y'understand. First thing we played was a letter I'd written called *Indigo Drizzle*. A modal riff with a little major-minor shift. It went nice. Felton was hawkin it rough. Billy was holdin his own. I had a nice thing goin, a rhythmic tease. We's cookin it slow and steady. Then in walks Lonnie. Boy had said he didn't want to even be there, not if he couldn't play. But there he was, still all swollen up from the dentist. Had his horn behind his back and whipped it out on about the eighth bar, during the bridge—and he jumped off. If you listen to the track—the album was called *My Appetite*—you can hear me start to say, 'No, don't...' But it was too late. Lonnie was blowin. Blood comin off his lips, right down his face. Then it was just flowin. But he kept blowin. I couldn't stand to watch it, but I couldn't take my eyes off him. Blood sprayin out his horn. He never stopped playin. When it was Felton's solo, LB harmonized underneath, then he took another solo. The blood was all on his face and down his shirt and he kept blowin. We had to rename that track. It wasn't an *Indigo Drizzle* now. We called it *Spontaneous Combustion*...Man! Never shoulda got in that car with Billy Heron. Never shoulda...Goddamn! We had rules in that band," Red muttered, and it caught me off guard, and I forgot myself—or maybe I'd just had enough.

"What the hell are you talking about?" I said.

"I'm speakin about Billy Heron, man. Wish I knew what happened to it. Lonnie's ticket, his train ticket. He was supposed to take the train with us, but lost his ticket. Ended up in the car with Billy and that woman. We had rules, man. You ain't a solo act. Supposed to follow the damn rules."

"Did you follow the rules?" I asked, and he raised his head. "You don't seem to mind letting a woman drive a car now so you can get a free lunch and a haircut and some stogies.

So why you gotta spit on the grave of the man you played alongside?"

Red shook his head to himself, then he squashed the lit end of the cigar under his orthopedic shoe. He was pale. He said to no one in particular: "We ain't on the road now. And why is she pickin up for Billy Heron?"

"Because she's Billy Heron's daughter."

Red tilted his head, sideways and spied at me through half-closed eyes. "You for real?"

"I'm Didi Heron."

"I thought you said you was from a record company. Alamode."

"Don't mean I ain't got a father."

He got sad and very quiet. Stayed quiet for a long time. When he finally spoke it was barely a whisper passing between his lips. "Billy was your father?"

"He still is," I said, and Red turned away.

He said, "Don't be mad at Red Young. Please, don't be mad."

"Tell me how he played. That night at The Sound Box. I want you to tell me about the way Billy Heron played that last gig."

"Damn good, he played damn good."

"I don't believe you. I don't believe you believe it."

"I didn't like him. He didn't like me, but it's true. He was *on* that night. I don't know what happened. We was all on fire, but yeah, especially him. He was the man. You have to understand. He didn't like me and I didn't like him and that is just the way it was and can't nothin change that." He turned back around, studying my face, shaking his head. "I thought I saw somethin in you, somethin that brought it all back." He kept shaking his head. "Man, oh, man…"

"Damn you!" came a voice from outside the room. After a moment of fumbling on the other side of the doorway, it opened. Carlton stood staring in. "Leave my friend alone!"

"No," I said. "You get out of here."

"He's weeping," Carlton said. "You had no right to get his hopes up."

"It's none of your business."

"I'm his friend."

"So am I," I said.

"That's a lie. He's sobbing like a baby because of you. "

I looked over at Red, waiting for him to say something, but he just sat on his bed, staring at a photograph of his granddaughter.

"You get out of here," Carlton said.

"This is not your room," I said.

"You're a threat to his health. I'm calling the manager." Carlton took a step back into the hallway.

"Wait."

"Why should I?"

And all I could think of was: "Because I need you both to record a tape. I want your new sound. I want to play it for my boss. He'll be in L.A. next week. He's anxious to hear it. Have you got a recorder?"

The man was all flustered. "Actually, the fact of the matter is that I don't. But you say you need it by next week?"

"That's right."

"And what company did you say you were with?"

"Alamode, but we're part of the GLX family of labels."

"Don't they put out Vienna Records? That's who should release our sound. It isn't jazz, not really. It's an amalgamation, you see, a new form. It deserves to be treated with great seriousness."

"I'm sure it will be."

"And I won't have you cheating us either." Carlton added. "Our music is revolutionary. You pay top dollar for it or we go elsewhere!"

"I'll warn Nils Tanner."

"You do that," he said.

Red was back in the world again. He said, "I'm glad to see my friends gettin along. Life too short to hold a grudge."

Monday morning, I was back on the highway, heading west to L.A. with Red in the passenger seat, holding a cassette he and Carlton had made with a blind resident's Grundig deck.

We were silent for most of the ride, which seemed a lot shorter than the ride out there almost three weeks ago. I branched off I-10 to avoid the desolation of shopping malls and billboards and gas station signs. The 60 took us through some hills, brown with green patches, and as we neared L.A., I picked up the jazz station, KBCA, playing *Nica's Dream*, the slow tempo version, Horace Silver with Donald Byrd and Hank Mobley. Then Red rescued me from my thoughts, remembering, out loud, the night he sat in with Horace. "It was at an old theater in Vinegar Hill, The Quarter Note. Horace was a drummer on the piano, y'understand. If you were goin to keep time for him, you had to really give it some kick. If you were goin to play the horn with him, you had to have built-in soul. Still do, man, still do, 'cause that brotha is still goin strong. But that's not what I wanted to say. See, what I'm tryin to say is me and Horace had a talk between sets that night. Horace, man, he was *clean* in his fur coat and cap and toked an *un*filtered cigarette. Told me there was a rhythm to everything—every livin piece of life—got a heartbeat. Every time the wind blow it is changin the tempo. Ocean waves and the planetary rotations, they the most senior members of the drum corps. And the world's problems, man, could mostly be attributed to a situation gettin off tempo, sticks out of alignment. Said the job of the drummer was to realign things. Can you dig it?"

"Uh-huh," I chanted. "Yes, I can most certainly dig that."

"We friends now, Miss Didi Heron?"

"Yeah, we're friends now, Mr. Red Young."

From the outside, the Hollywood GLX recording studio looked like an abandoned building—except that there was a parking lot next to it with about six Mercedes, a few Porches, and a Bentley. An armed guard sat on a metal stool protecting them. Inside the building was clean and cold with carpet so thick you got a shock touching every door handle. Red was impressed. "Man," he said, "seems like jazz got dignity round here." Then we reached studio 5, where Nils had told us to meet him. He knew Red was coming and I had told him why. A red light was on above the studio door, meaning they were recording. A hand-written arrow on a piece of lined paper pointed us to the engineer's booth entrance where we found Nils in tennis shorts and a polo shirt sitting at a console along with a bearded guy in blue jeans and two dudes in suits. Through a speaker we heard a funky-sounding fusion tune, electric bass and guitars, Fender Rhodes, steady, mechanical high-hat, buttery alto sax. I looked through the large soundproof glass and saw a pair of musicians and about five synthesizers. They were jamming, man and machine, but what Red whispered I had to agree with, "Where's the soul, man? Where's the people?"

Nils saw Red and called for a lunch break and introduced Red Young to the other guys in the booth. They took turns pumping Red's hand and that seemed to make Red very satisfied. Nils told them to leave us alone, and had Red sit next to him at the board. I leaned on the edge of a table behind them.

"It's an honor to meet you," Nils said.

"I feel the same way meeting you, sir."

"Call me Nils. Please. I remember when cats like you were adding and subtracting and changing the landscape as you played."

"Thank you for saying that."

"You played with Charlie Parker for a short time, didn't you?"

"Back then, everybody played with everybody."

"Were you with Bird at The Last Door, May 8th, 1951?"

Red gave his sideways shrug, then a nod. "Yes, I believe so. Max Roach was preoccupied that night if I am not mistaken."

"You're the unknown drummer."

"Excuse me?"

Nils got up from his seat and reached for a large leather brief case, and from it removed a shiny LP jacket. It was called *Fresh Bird (Previously Unreleased and Live), Volume 3*. Nils showed Red the reverse side, noting the personnel and where the various recordings had taken place. I leaned over to watch Nils point to three tunes recorded at The Last Door. Charlie Parker on alto, Duke Jordan on piano, guitar unknown, bass unknown, drums unknown."

Red let off a smile. "That was me. Bass was Leroy Chones. Guitar, that was—I think—must have been Charlie Pilcher."

Nils relished the exchange and that got me jealous in a crazy way.

"Would you sign it?" Nils asked, handing Red a pen.

"Should he sign it Red Young or Unknown?" I asked.

Nils didn't answer. Red didn't seem to hear.

Nils showed Red where to sign, and Red obliged. Then Nils said, "Think I'll call my friend at Stash Records and tell him to get the names right on here for the next printing."

"I do appreciate that," Red told him. "Now, I'd like to tell you about my new sound."

"Absolutely."

"It's me and my man, Carlton. Carlton Von Schmidt. He was a composer on..." Red tried to remember.

"Oh, you don't have to tell me. I know his music. And you're collaborating—that's wonderful."

Red held up the cassette.

"Let's hear it."

Red handed it over. Nils swiveled in his chair and popped it into a deck behind us.

We listened.

I was amazed at the energy in the music from these two old men. Still, the music itself was worse than I'd remembered.

Disjointed, atonal, rambling, like Carlton's stomach noises set to music. But as awful as it was, I thought Nils should have let the two old men make an album of it. How much would it cost? Worse recordings have been pressed into vinyl. I watched Nils. He seemed intrigued.

"What do you call it?" he asked.

Red shrugged. "Don't know. Got any ideas?"

"I couldn't even begin."

"You like it?"

"It's got many possibilities. May I hold onto the tape for a while?"

"Yes, sir."

"I think it's great you're still making music," Nils told him. "How come you dropped out of the scene for so long?"

"Nils!"

"I'm sure he has his reasons," Nils said, without looking at me.

"Yeah, you could say that," Red agreed.

"If it's a sensitive thing, I understand."

"He had a family to support," I said. "And club dates and record deals don't have much financial security. Who wants to raise kids around all that cigarette smoke and drugs and liquor and what have you?"

"Got that right," Red agreed.

"Yeah," Nils said, ever the diplomat. "Who can argue with that?" Then he added: "I can't wait to hear our other tape."

"Other tape?"

Nils grinned, winked at me, and I wondered if I seemed, to Red, as callous as Nils right now seemed to me.

"I'm talking about the Lonnie Baylor tape," Nils said. "Or has Didi made it up?"

"Ain't nobody made it up," Red assured.

"I'm sorry," Nils said. "I didn't mean—"

"I'm starting to think I know where it is," Red offered. "You know, I have trouble remembering and I think it's 'cause I spend all my damn time out there in the desert. Too much dry air not good for the mind, I think. Gettin away from there's given me a new perspective on things. Yeah, I got an idea where I ought to be lookin for that tape."

"Where's that?" Nils asked.

"Muriel. My sister. She live in Milwaukee. I went to stay with her right after I came from LB's funeral in Chicago."

"Can you have your sister look?"

"She's an old woman. Got a three story house and the tape's probably in the attic."

Nils said, "Excuse me," and took me outside the sound booth and onto the sound stage. The musicians were gone now but one of the synthesizers was still droning at us as Nils whispered in my ear: "What do you think? You think he's for real about the sister having it?"

No, I didn't believe it at all. More likely the old guy wanted an all expenses paid trip to visit her. "Yeah," I whispered back to Nils, "I think we ought to go."

Chapter Seven:

How High the Blue Moon

Back in Rancho Mirage, before Red and I hit the road, I called my mother to ask if we had any relatives in the Milwaukee area who I might visit while I was there, but the closest Mom could come up with were some cousins in Detroit.

She was worried, as always, about me getting on an airplane. But I assured her that I would remain very much earthbound; Red Young had us on the Amtrak—had to feel the steady beat beneath his feet.

"Red Young," My mother mused. "I don't think he liked your father very much."

"That's all in the past."

"That's what I'm saying," she said, which pretty much ended the conversation.

I didn't sleep much that night before we left, half-thoughts like bumper cars. It was already hot at seven-thirty the next morning when I checked out of the motel and drove to Steiner Hall. Red was on a wooden bench just inside the lobby. He was bundled in slacks and a dress shirt that fit him like a sleeping bag. A blank baseball cap flopped to one side on his head.

"Ready to go?" I asked.

Red nodded yes. He reached for a tiny old pink suitcase at the end of the bench.

"You sure you packed enough?" I asked.

"No, I'm not," he said.

"Would you like me to help?"

"Let's just go."

"Not so fast." Carlton emerged from behind the Max Steiner statue. He wore bright yellow satin pajamas, had a sleeping mask propped on his forehead. "You deceived us!" he cried. He got up in my face with his metallic breath.

"I'll be back soon," Red told Carlton, stepping between us.

"I won't be here when you get back."

"Where you gonna be?"

"In the ground."

"Man, quit that shit. Don't nobody believe it, and don't nobody wanna hear it."

"You'll see."

"Man, you die and I'm gonna make that album and won't give you a damn bit of credit."

"I'll sue you. I'll have my estate sue you."

"You ain't got no estate, boy."

"You be careful out there with that gal," Carlton said.

"She's good people," Red said and reached out to his friend.

Carlton brought his arm up and the two men danced together in an unsteady embrace, then Red joined me in the doorway and I carried that little pink suitcase to the car. "You know," he said getting in, "that man, Carlton, was a genius. Prodigy, they called him. Wrote a whole symphony when he was ten years old. You know what a symphony is?" Red asked.

"Yes, I know."

Carlton was behind us, had followed us outside, one hand up. I couldn't tell if it was trembling or waving from side to side.

There was a Hertz office across Indian Avenue from the Palm Springs Amtrak station. An agent checked the Dart in and made arrangements for us to get another midsize in Milwaukee.

My duffle bag strap pulled my head to one side as I led the way onto the station platform. Red carried his own suitcase. His limp had a little bounce, almost like a strut. We stared down the shiny tracks in the dry heat. Sounded like buzzards in the distance waiting for us to dry up and get crispy. We could see our Texas Eagle double-decker from far away, rounding the edge of the ragged foothills. Red was excited to be getting on a train.

"Man, oh man," he said at the luxury of the first class sleeper car, the wide cloth bench, the brass ashtrays and deep wood paneling. Not to mention the wide window to the world between here and Wisconsin.

The train lurched into its forward roll and I leaned back in my seat. Through the window, I watched the faces of a few people waving goodbye. I glanced over at Red, who was already napping furiously. I closed my eyes and let my head fall onto my shoulder. When I woke up, we were still in the desert. Red was awake and staring at cacti and boulders speeding by. He had a Coke with a cherry in it. He was talking, and I wasn't sure if he somehow knew, without looking, that I'd awakened, or if he was talking to himself:

"Dallas wasn't like this. Not quite, but it reminds me in a way."

"Reminds you of what?" I asked.

"You have a nice nap?"

"Yes, thanks. What does it remind you of?" I craved a remembrance against the desolate landscape.

"We was there for Eddie Barnett's funeral."

"Tell me about it."

"Eddie Barnett—band leader. Nineteen-fifty. Most everyone played for Eddie one time or other. Dusty old cemetery they buried him. Bunch a sad relatives. Kids running around. When they were all gone, we all stayed on. Didn't feel like going to a party and being looked at. You see, the family, they will sometimes blame the musicians. So there we were—and we stomped, we carved the rock, y'understand, we did a cemetery jam. And don't go askin me if anybody had a tape recorder 'cause I got to say that was the last thing on anybody's mind. Man, we ain't thinkin no one would ever be payin to hear what we was playin that day. Musta had four trumpets, seven saxophones. I ain't had a kit and neither did Kenny—Kenny Clarke—but we had a beat goin with some stick action on Eddie's tomb stone. Wake the sucka up!"

"A jazz funeral," I said. "In the true sense."

"It was really somethin. But you know what? There was too many, way too many jazz funerals, and didn't need to be. What we needed was some jazz weddings, some jazz baptisms, you know. More of the happy."

I nodded my head with him. "But what did you play, at the jazz funeral?"

"How I'm supposed to remember that?"

"What *do* you remember?"

"We played *Cherokee.* Played it like I never heard before or since."

"What did it sound like?"

"Can't describe it. Swung it like an Indian waltz."

I could hear it in my mind and I could feel it, suddenly. Like I was there. I felt myself playing with them, hearing my sound. I was the fifth trumpet.

"We was a bluesifying machine, y'understand," Red went on. "That's right. Took the changes to *Come Rain or Come Shine* and made it *The Come Rain or Come Shine Blues*, took *Tea for Two* and made it *The Tea for One Blues* then put *How High the Moon* together with *Blue Moon* and made *How High The Blue Moon.* Musta been two, three hours till the police got there. Separated us by race. Wasn't sure where to put my light skinned self. Kenny Clarke told me to head with the white cats, so they'd have a drummer. And we played for the cops' too. They made us do the Texas anthem and a Glenn Miller tune in a cold cell smelled like burnt margarine. Later on I found out the cops made the black musicians do the same thing, only I heard someone kept interjecting slave songs."

I could hear it all and pictured myself there and my father too, jamming on a toy piano, like the one he'd bought for me a few months before the accident, like the one I saw Derrick play at Paragon House—Daddy cooking on those two tiny octaves.

The steady beat was the locomotion beneath us and the rhythm of Red's voice, reeling me into his memories, making them somehow my own. Naturally, I would have preferred more stories that included Billy Heron, but I didn't push. I was still wary of what might come out of Red's mouth if I mentioned my father's name, so instead I invited Dad along myself, secretly.

Palm Springs to Milwaukee was a long ride—eight states on two trains in three days. I sponge-bathed and changed my clothes each day, but by the third day I began to feel a rancid film coating me. I needed some air that hadn't been re-circulated through a vent. Needed to talk about plans, not just memories. But I thought I ought to keep Red looking backwards, so our last morning on that train, as we sat in the dining car speeding past the outskirts of Chicago, the city where LB had been buried, I asked about that funeral.

"Nothin much to talk about." Red's eyes were set off in the distance at some ugly factories and a green haze, then wide-open space and a jagged horizon. Glasses of orange grapefruit juice arrived, along with the hickory smell of food heading for someone else's table. "I don't know. Too many too soon departures, man." Red glanced off at a wrecking yard, automobile carcasses piled high. "Didn't make no sense to no one. Even Diz, man. He brought a jar of peanut butter along to LB's funeral. Was gonna have some fun. See, LB used to always eat nut butter out the jar and always had that smell on him, and Diz, I think, was gonna spread some on the preacher in LB's honor. But when it come time, he didn't have the spirit. Nobody did. First Eddie Barnett, then we done buried Fats Navarro, then Bird, now LB—and Billy," he added, and I appreciated it, even as an afterthought. "Like there's a curse gonna get us all. Lotta drinkin that weekend. Lotta poppin off, too, man. That was the crime of it. That LB was the man to look to. An example. He made his music without that shit. Proved you could do it. But his death made people want to just shoot some shit. Just too damn sad."

This time I didn't want to live inside Red's recollection, but I couldn't stop the drift. Inside that memory, I saw everything through the net of a black veil, saw a towering old Baptist church, gray stone outside, then inside, the rows of varnished benches, floor and balcony, decked-out people squeezed in, the forlorn faces of Red Young and Felton Payne and John Birks "Dizzy" Gillespie, as they carried the box. Then I saw the backs of their hatted heads. I was LB's fourth pallbearer and the weight, in this imagined memory, was almost too much for me. On the front steps, icy snow crunched under foot and made a slight romp but no one seemed to notice. We loaded the casket inside a black Cadillac hearse, and then suddenly I was at a different funeral and I was much smaller and without the veil. I hadn't remembered it for a long time, that moment when they lowered Daddy into the ground. Something so horrifying in the final moment of a father never coming back. I kept thinking about him under the ground, all by himself, away from me, away from Mommy, just laying in a box in the ground. What had he done to deserve being all alone forever like that?

"You all right?" Red asked. "Hey."

"I'm fine!" In my reverie, I must have shouted—people were staring.

Red's eggs arrived, then my French toast. Our juice glasses got refilled.

Red slid a fried egg onto a slice of toast and said, "I got to talk to you about my sister. She's a stubborn old woman. I love her but I've stayed away for good reason. Don't get into no serious conversations with Muriel. You will regret it."

It was a balmy afternoon in Milwaukee, the sky gray. My duffle seemed to have gotten heavier, and the weight made me limp almost as much as Red.

"You know how to get to your sister's house?" I asked, leaning on the Hertz counter

"Not far from the station, I do believe," Red said. He slouched next to me, and couldn't seem to keep his eyes on anything for very long.

In an adjacent garage, I matched the license plate of a blue Omega with the numbers attached to my set of Oldsmobile keys and heaved my duffle into the trunk, then eased Red's suitcase in next to it and opened the passenger side door for him. But Red did not get in. "I'll drive," he said. "We're on the road now."

I didn't argue. I had done a lot of driving these past weeks—more than I'd ever done before—and needed a break.

Red settled himself into the driver's seat. He tried to move it forward but instead made it lean back, then he pushed the knob the other way and seemed to get a slight whiplash from the sudden forward movement. The side mirrors confused him for a while, then he started her up with a slow twist and a hard push on the gas pedal, as if trying to awaken that engine from the dead. He maneuvered it out of the parking lot then steered casually onto a street and drifted three lanes over without looking. Cars honked at us from all directions, and I sank low and tried not to watch. I think we were going the wrong way down a one-way street. Red winced, shook his head at the audacity of all the other drivers. Then he got his bearings, somewhat, and made a left onto another street, going with the flow. We drove past breweries-turned-nightclubs and the skeletons of abandoned tenements beautified with vibrant murals. Then he drove under a freeway and came to a dead end. He spun a U-turn and went on. A few blocks down, he stopped at a large intersection. His eyes drooped and his breathing became choppy.

"Why don't you let me drive?"

Red answered impatiently: "I told you already. Rules is rules. Damn good rules. Number one: no narcotics or any kind of serious drinking. Even Felton—boy was clean for the whole time we all was a quintet. Rule two: no selling charts to other groups. Number three: don't mess with nobody else's woman. And four: don't ever let no lady behind the wheel of a car!"

Stupid bullshit, but I let it go.

Red stopped the car in front of a three-story Victorian house that had been turned into an apartment building, painted bright green with dark trim. "There it is," he said. "Used to all be her own, way back when. Now, she just has half the top floor. That's what she say."

I hopped out of the car, grabbed Red's suitcase from the trunk, and started for the front door.

"What about your bag?" Red asked from behind.

"I saw a Holiday Inn a few blocks back," I told him.

"Stay here."

"I can't invite myself."

"I'm inviting you," Red said.

"It's not your house." Truth was, I needed a break—from Red's voice and from the cayenne smell of his skin and the lime smell of his hair tonic and the stale odor of his opinions. I needed some quiet. Needed to gather myself.

"I can't face that woman alone," he said.

"She's your sister."

"I need a friend."

I got my bag out of the trunk and followed him up a wooden stairway to the top floor doorway. I did the knocking for him, then stepped to the side. A moment later, the door opened and there was a scream from inside and Red was enfolded by a pair of thick arms. For a moment, he disappeared completely, then seemed to be vacuum-sucked in through the doorway. I tried to follow.

Red's sister got in my way. She was built like a vending machine. Large oval glasses framed a pair of squinting hazel eyes.

"Yes?"

"I'm with Red."

"You his caretaker?"

"No."

"You his woman?"

"I'm a business associate."

"That's right," Red chimed in.

Muriel looked me over, then let me inside, but even then it was a tight squeeze. Too much furniture and too many artifacts. A pretty sculpture of the sun, another of the moon, a waterfall, Jesus on the cross. Walls covered with portraits of Baby Jesus and Martin Luther King and of a young man in an army uniform trying to smile.

I followed Red's sister through a narrow corridor to a sitting room with faded flags-of-the-world wallpaper and an old buffed-to-a-sparkle church organ. I sat next to Red on a corduroy sofa. He kept glancing around in amazement. "My little sis," he said, pressing his lips together and shaking his head.

"How long has it been, Joshua?"

"A long time," Red answered. "Too long for family."

"Whose choice was that?"

"Let's not speak on that." Red scratched at something on the right knee of his pants, a stain he'd picked up somewhere between California and this house.

"I'm happy to see you, my brother. I believed that one day I would hear word that you had died, and I wouldn't know if you'd gotten salvation."

"My little sis."

"Why did you stay away?" she asked.

"Let's not."

"Let's not what?"

"Let's not. Let's just—"

"Let's go out to dinner," I suggested. "My treat."

It took a while for Muriel to prepare herself for the restaurant, and during that time, Red and I snuck up to the attic, sneezing dust and hacking at cobwebs and fanning ourselves with old crumbling sheets of shirt cardboard from rotting men's shirts. We rummaged and scavenged. We found five photographs of Red going back to his boyhood in St. Louis. He looked like a happy kind of impatient child. One photo showed him licking ice cream. Some was on his nose. Another photo showed him and his sister hugging, their eyes closed, their baby teeth grinning at one another. More photos. The young soldier again.

"That was Calvin," Red said. "My brother-in-law. He died at Normandy."

There were old magazines. *National Enquirers* crammed into a box with a publication called *His Voice*. A box of dance records, mired in mouse droppings.

Muriel came creaking up the stairs, shouting, "What in the world! You two up there in my attic?"

"Looking at the old pictures," Red said.

Muriel stood on the attic ladder, her face level with the floor. "It's filthy up there."

"We all right," Red told her. "I left some things up here last time."

"But you ain't been here since…"

"But I am now."

"Yes, I remember now," Muriel said. "You were wearing a suit with a wilted flower. You had come from a funeral." She pronounced it fee-yune-rul.

"I had a tape with me—a tape recording—at least I believe I did."

"Satan was a guest at that funeral."

"Please, Muriel. Please, little sis. Don't say those things."

"And wanted to drag a buncha your heathen friends in here."

"Just tell me, li'l sis. Was there a tape? Recorded tape, I mean. Did you find a box, about so big, with a reel of magnetic tape inside?"

"Find it where?"

"Up here. Or anyplace else in this house?"

"I don't remember no tapes."

"You sure?"

"And if they were tapes of the devil music, I'd have thrown them out any old way."

"Why you gotta talk that mess?"

"Those eleven and thirteenth chords, they are the music of Lucifer's parade!" she shouted up toward us. "And crazy sounding satanic meter. Thank God you stopped playing it! Oh, yes, I remember when all you could do was accompany the devil's theme song. Praise the Lord you got away from it; got it out of your system. That's why you come back to visit Muriel. But don't ever underestimate Satan. He is always waiting on you." She pointed a finger toward us. "You and you and everyone. He's been working on me, trying my whole life."

"Please stop that talk!" Red shouted through the attic door. "Let's go to dinner, my little sis." And he led the way down the narrow attic stairs.

We got in the car and drove. I wasn't sure where in Milwaukee to find a restaurant worthy of Muriel's red dress and matching hat and her hefty string of pearls—but when we passed a Black Angus, she asked if we could eat there.

In the restaurant, Red sat across from me, next to Muriel who ordered steak and shrimp. That sounded good so I ordered the same. Red got himself a T-bone.

"You going to stay for awhile?" Muriel asked while we waited for our food.

"Don't know," Red told her. "I really have to find that tape."

"I told you I destroyed them. You should thank me."

"You said you weren't sure."

"Consider'em gone and you be a whole lot better off."

"You're right, sis. I know you're right."

"His Will be done. I know these things."

I tried to gauge Red—afraid, suddenly, that I'd lost him. He chewed ice for a while, till his T-bone arrived, then sliced it thin like bacon. Muriel said grace, louder than was comfortable for some customers at the tables around us. Some people stopped eating and bowed their heads and then stared at her when it was over. Muriel savored every bite, spread butter on her meat.

"I know about these things," she said to me. "I studied music just like Red. Nobody believed I was anything special—but I was the real musician around here. I've sang in the choir for thirty-eight years and played the organ every other Sunday. I've written original hymns. God is the only band leader of merit and He wants me in *His* orchestra."

"You can count on that. My little sis." He reached over and stroked her cheek.

"Not too late for you, my brother."

Red grinned. "Hey, I tell you one thing, if God's got an orchestra up there, he don't need a drummer with all that thunder and what not."

I laughed. Muriel did not. She repeated, "Not too late. Not ever too late for you or you, young lady."

"You're wrong about Lonnie," Red told her.

"Excuse me?"

"What I'm sayin is I don't doubt God has an orchestra up there, but he must also have a jazz band. I know it because Lonnie Baylor ain't in no kinda hell. Oh, no. You didn't know him, sis. You didn't know him."

"I didn't need to."

"He used to mop up the floor at The Onyx."

"Mopping don't get you into heaven."

"See there was an old janitor gone blind from his cataracts. Worked at The Onyx and didn't tell the boss. Would mop up like he could still see what he was doin. Only he'd miss about half the floor and step all over where he'd just cleaned. LB seen him gettin cussed out by the boss one night, talkin bout you're gonna be fired. That night on, LB went and mopped up after him. Did it for a year even when we'd be playin way uptown somewhere, he'd ride the A-train straight down to The Onyx afterwards and mop. Would use the toilet bowl for a bucket. Just to save the man his job. Lonnie was a good man. So was this girl's father, Billy Heron, who was also in that car."

"That's just it," Muriel said, mashing butter into her baked potato. "Devil prefers to corrupt good men."

"You have to understand what he did for me. Lonnie was just a kid when I first heard him play. Barely eighteen. It was a Sunday night on 52nd Street. At a club that went out of business the next week. Called itself Upstairs In The Back. Couldn't nobody ever find it. Whole house band got chickenpox and I got the call to fill in. Trumpet player showed up was Lonnie Baylor, fresh off the bus, I swear. We was out of work in four days, but kept in touch. I'd recommend LB for a gig or he'd do the same. Didn't realize how great he was at the time 'cause he was modest, didn't want to show up anyone. Then my man Felton got out of prison where he musta written a hundred tunes. High energy charts, smokin quintet ammunition. Next thing we had a band. Don't know how Billy Heron landed on piano or Cole on the bass. I believe they just met LB at some sessions and he liked them. That was all it took. We cooked, man, from day one. Called ourselves the Jazz Prophets, but Kenny Dorham had a group by that same name, and by the time we got around to changin ours the world had discovered LB and we was the LB Quintet, which was fine. Felton was also startin to make his mark, and we was bein billed as the LB Quintet Featuring Felton Payne. Point is, LB and Felt was way above my head, really. I was the heartbeat but LB coulda had himself any drummer on the scene. Kenny Clarke, Max Roach, Philly Jo. Any of'em. But he stuck by me." Red looked fiercely at his little sister. "So don't you tell me he's in hell. Don't even say that."

Muriel lifted the napkin off her lap, soaked the tip in her water glass and offered it to Red, glancing down toward the stain on his pant leg. "Devil is the ultimate salesman. Isn't he, though? A smiling face. A generosity that lasts till it's over and too late. Too late and then…"

Red waved off Muriel's wet napkin, seemed now almost proud of his stain. He also waved off her invitation to spend the night. An hour later, Red and I were in the rented Omega, having deposited Muriel at her house. Red seemed to have trouble seeing, but wouldn't give up the wheel, and I didn't have the strength to get angry about it.

"You suppose there's a train leaving tonight?" I asked, though I wasn't sure where we might be going.

Red seemed oblivious. He kept hanging rights, an occasional left and squinting through the windshield at the glare of headlights and street lamps. He squeaked and whistled a tune that was unrecognizable to me, then spoke, punctuating each phrase with his foot on the break. First he said: "I'm sorry about what I said."

"About what?"

"About Billy. Your father. I'm sorry I ever said a bad word about him. Can you forget about it?"

"I already have."

"Thank you," he said, his voice cracking. "That night at The Sound Box. LB's last. Shit—*my* last. Man, that was my *mission*. To preserve and deliver that tape so the music could live."

"It's all right," I told him. "You tried. That's all you can do."

"I'm the only living member in that quintet. Only one reason I'm still alive is to find that tape. Need to be heard. God—talkin bout the Bebop God, not that gospel-loving God Muriel be talkin about—the Bebop God, He keepin me here for one reason."

Chapter Eight:

Later Crocodilia

Red asked if we could call his son, Lou, in Ohio. We were so close and would it be too far out of our way?

"You think maybe your son knows where the tape is?"

Red played along, or maybe he really believed it: "His garage. Could be."

We found a payphone on the sidewalk outside the rental car office. Moonbeams trembled across long clouds above our heads. The moon itself was hidden by a towering clock. I stood close to Red, listening at his insistence. He grasped at my arm as he spoke hoarsely. "Hello, son?"

"Pop!" His son's voice spat hard out of the receiver.

"Who you thought it was?" Red asked him.

I heard his son say: "Aunt Muriel called me, Pop. Where are you?"

"I'm in a parking lot. Bout to leave Milwaukee."

"You and that woman?" the son asked.

"Ain't nobody said anything about a woman!"

"Aunt Muriel told me."

"You know how Muriel is."

"Pop, if you got a lady, I'm down with that. Just be careful. Like you used to tell me."

"You forgive me, son?" Red asked.

"Pop, now don't go taking credit for messing up my life."

Red let a beat pass. "I need to come see you."

"Right now?" Lou asked.

"I can be in Cleveland by the morning."

"I'd love to see you, Pop, but it's still not a good time."

Red nodded silently into the phone.

"Pop?"

I grabbed the receiver and spoke into it: "Look, this is not a social call. I'm with a record company. Mr. Young and I are trying to find some of his property that my company wishes to purchase. This is very important. He thinks it might be in your possession."

To no one in particular, Red yelled, "Never mind!"

"No, wait!" Lou shouted. "Tell Pop I'm sorry. I'll meet you at the airport."

"Train station," I told him.

"Get off before Cleveland!" Red's son told me. "I live in Port Clay."

There were no berths available for us on the 10:26 Lakeshore Limited, so we stretched out on a pair of coach seats amidst the tired murmuring of late-night conversations punctuated by laughter and snoring. The railroad tracks hugged the lake for a while and I watched the flickering lights of boats that seemed not to be moving. Red was looking out the same window in the same direction, but didn't seem to be seeing the same things or anything in particular. Vaguely, I saw him nod in the reflection off the glass and with that he said:

"You know, what I can remember quite clearly is the greatest days. What it was for me. No particular time, y'understand. Sometime right before the end of the war. Helen and me. Man! You don't know. I can remember what it felt like to be apart, knowin we'd be together later on that night, knowin I'd tiptoe in on Lou in his little bed, listen to the boy mumble in his sleep and watch him roll around and make a big old crease on his pudgy little mug. Or sometimes he'd wake up and we'd talk. Boy always had a million questions. I composed a letter around that time, about those moments with Lou. What I named it, can't recall, but I can hear that melody still. Can hear all the music me and the fellas were playin and the feelin it had, that very sweet feelin of playin on the outside. Do you know what I mean?"

"I'm not sure," I said.

"On the outside," he said again. "Nobody even wanted to cut a bebop record, those first few years, you know: '44, '45. Couldn't dance to it anyway. Folks called it a bastard music. You wanted to hear bop, had to be inside with the musical outlaws, y'understand? You had to be right there to hear the impulse of acoustic instrumentality inventin more electricity than Niagara Falls. Funny thing. It was those couple few years—between the birth of the Bop and the day Dizzy and Bird played on the television—that we had the best times. I ain't just sayin that because these years coincided with when I was in love in that way where you're talkin tender and makin love hot, or because Lou was a little boy and still sweet and lookin up to me. Times were not easy. Money was tight. Many nights I brought home salt peanuts from the club for dinner. Helen had a miscarriage and a stillborn during those years. But the music, the ecstasy in each riff, and me keepin time, I was ridin a wave that was pushin against musical gravity. While that cat, Oppenheimer, and his scientists invented the A-bomb, we invented the A-flat bomb. That's the feelin I miss most. And you know what? Nowadays, it pains Red Young just a little bit to see a cat from back then on TV, wearin a tuxedo and collectin an award. Ain't jealousy. Hell no. I love those boys and want to see them get recognized. But it's always some square-headed somebody handin out the statue or makin the speech, someone who ain't never appreciated bop back when, and has no business now stickin an arm 'round a musical outlaw like we all brothas in this."

Our train turned away from the lake and a curtain of darkness pressed against the windows. Red closed his eyes and his head slumped against his shoulder. I had to make myself sleep and couldn't find a dream to hold on to. Morning came quickly. We were back along the shore with the rising sun drawing a white snake down the choppy width of Lake Erie. Soon the train rattled into the Port Clay station. Red and I carried ourselves out onto the landing and down to the platform. The station was made of old wood and gray brick. Red didn't seem to recognize anyone in there. Then a voice, big and smooth, echoed: "Pop! Hey, Pop! Over here."

The voice came from a side entrance and the man filled it with his husky frame and his high-standing, half-receding fro. As he walked out of a shadow and into the station light his grainy complexion seemed to darken. He lifted Red off the floor with a hug, laughed at the old pink suitcase, and picked it up. "You're looking good, Pop!" He smiled at me, and I tensed away from him, wouldn't let him take my duffle bag. He snatched it away from me, tossing the bag over his shoulder. Lou's free arm squeezed Red, and Red rested his head on his son's shoulder. I followed behind, admiring their affection. Automatic glass doors swung open and Lou led the way to his green Trans Am.

Lou's driving was more reckless than his father's. The younger Young sped out of the parking lot without bothering to find the driveway. He lurched over the curb, made an impossible left onto a highway, cut through a shopping mall parking lot at forty to avoid an intersection. I braced myself against the worn leather backseat and tried to distract myself with a glossy magazine from a side pocket, but it was just page after page of men's clothing advertised on unshaven models. Lou turned the radio to a station which announced itself as "WPYF. Playing your faves in Northeastern Ohio." Then came Stevie Wonder's *Boogie on Reggae Woman*, followed by The Bee Gees shrieking about: "You should be dancing!" A DJ came on, his low voice rattling the car's back speakers: "Oh, yes, say it again and again, we all *should* be dancing. Still Number One, Bee Gees and right before that, Mr. Wonderful himself with a message we should all take to heart: it's summer, so let's party!"

"That boy sounds a little like you," Red said.

"That is me, Pop. On delay."

Just then, Lou's voice announced, "It's six forty-eight in the a.m. and a cool sixty-five," and Lou cringed as we passed a bank's electronic time and temp, which confirmed 6:48, but then said it was now 72 degrees.

Stopped at an intersection, Lou told his father: "Reyna said it was all right if we stop by before Anya goes to school."

"I don't want to bother her."

"Sure you do, Pop. She's all you ever ask about."

In a few minutes we were parked in front of a red brick colonial. Lou pushed on the horn until the front door opened and out came a chubby girl in tight braids and purple sweats. She charged at the car and when Red opened his door and stepped out, she jumped onto him and squeezed him pale. Lou got out and caught his father before he fell against the side of the car. "How's my girl?" Red asked. Anya kept holding on and letting out that high-pitched squeal. Her eyes seemed to be looking out from some deep and confused place. Then she got quiet and stared up at a giant cloud in the sky and the wild energy drained out of her. She hung her right hand in front of her face and stared at her fingers, then touched them with the fingers of her left hand, as if trying to read Braille.

A woman followed her over to us. Big eyes like the girl and a red terrycloth robe. She put her cup of coffee up to her forehead and looked at me without saying anything, then pried the girl off her grandfather and dragged her back toward the house.

"Got to get ready for school, Anya," she said.

The girl shrieked and struggled, wailing the air with her fists.

For a moment I felt myself start toward them to help, but the woman—Anya's mother, I presumed—froze me with a look of contempt. I understood. It's like: where were you all last night or yesterday and where will you be tomorrow when this happens? I've put in time in special ed classrooms around New York. Not a lot—the city sub desk is careful not to burn anybody out—but enough to see that look on the faces of a few parents.

"You all right?" Lou asked.

"Me? I'm fine," I told him. I guess it did surprise me, though. All of Red's talk about his little girl. I kept picturing me on my dad's lap.

"She's autistic," Lou said.

"Must be tough," I said and noticed that Lou had the same sleepy eyelids as his father.

"Ain't nothin wrong with that child," Red yelled. "You *treat* her like she ain't right. That's all."

"Dad! Don't start."

"Girl got *spirit*!"

Anya's mother kept struggling with her until Red went over and lured her into the house with laughter and smiles. A few minutes later she was dressed and coming back out of the house with Red and her mom. Red's limp had become a bounce.

Lou got back in the driver's seat of his car and asked me which record label I worked for. When I told him Alamode he said he'd never heard of them but when I said it was part of the "GLX Family of Record Labels" he got all excited and said, "Oh, yeah. That's Village Records and Souldies." We small-talked it while Red and Anya waited for her school bus.

"I ought to thank you," Lou said. "Whoever you are and whatever you're doing with my dad, I've never seen him this happy."

"It's your daughter. He's crazy about her."

"I know my dad and this is the strongest I've seen him since my mom passed. And before that, too. Seemed like she barely kept him afloat. He was always all knotted up inside. My whole life anyway, as far back as I can remember. Grinding his jaw all day." Lou shook his head with what I was supposed to believe was amazement. "I wouldn't mind a little of whatever you're giving him."

"What the hell is that supposed to mean?"

He raised his hands in contrition.

"You think I'm getting down with your father?"

"No, nothing like that. I didn't mean—hey, don't take it the wrong way."

I glanced out at Red and his granddaughter as they stood at the curb, holding hands and watched the curving rise of the road. A short bus came slowly toward them, its dimensions distorted by the sloping angle of its approach.

Lou yawned and shifted in his driver's seat making the chapped vinyl groan. He stole a glance at me in his rearview mirror and seemed to be doing some silent calculations. "If Pop told you I never visit and I'm a no good lousy so and so, he's probably only slightly off."

I smiled. "No. Nothing like that."

"We used to live in L.A. Me and Rayna and Anya. Used to be a family. Anyway, my dad and me, wasn't ever much between us. He was so miserable all the time, since about the time I was twelve years old."

"Nineteen Fifty-six."

"Something like that. Used to cry right in front of me and never tell me why. Mom gave up a singing career for him. She had a beautiful voice. Used to sing to me so sweetly and tell me how lucky I was because Pop made a good living and I could go to Disneyland anytime I wanted. You see *your* dad a lot?"

"If my father was alive, I'd see him every chance I had."

"I'm sorry, I didn't know."

"Didn't your dad ever tell you what happened to his band?"

"Not really. Not much. You mean that trumpet player he knew?"

"And the piano player."

"Yeah, that's right, there were two."

"The piano player was my father."

"Your father—and my father? That make us cousins or something?"

Seemed like I ought to laugh at that. At least he was trying. I watched the sad little school bus pull up and Red coax Anya up the steps. Lou got out of the car and opened the door. His ex-wife stood a few feet away, waving to Anya through the window of the bus. Anya leaned out of a window and screamed what sounded like, "Later, crocodilia!"

Red hollered back to her, "Later, crocodilia!" And as the bus puttered away, he got in the front passenger seat of Lou's car and asked, "Why she gotta ride on that special bus? Ain't nothin wrong with that child."

Anya's mother kept her distance. She waved till the bus turned a corner, then walked back to her porch and went inside, screen door flapping behind her. Lou turned toward his father and said, "Lighten up, Pop. C'mon, I'll take you home. You'll get some sleep."

"She wants me to pick her up from school."

"How you gonna do that?" Lou asked.

"We'll rent a car," I said, and a few minutes later we were at an Alamo counter getting ourselves a Chevy Vega. Then Red and I followed Lou to his apartment building, a high rise with shiny white bricks and blue terraces facing Lake Erie.

Lou's pad was cool and clean, with white carpet and ultra-clean teak and Lucite furniture. A giant tropical fish tank sat on a white marble pedestal. Bright neon clowns zigzagging a steady string of bubbles from a shimmering treasure chest in water lit to ever changing colors. Beyond the tank, tinted windows overlooked a line of trees and beyond it the lake. Red flopped down on a futon sofa.

"You gonna be all right?" I asked.

"Don't worry about me."

I reached for the phone. "Where's a decent hotel around here?"

Lou took the phone from me. "This is family. You can have my room."

"No, thanks."

"Pop'll sleep in my study. I'll sleep outside on the terrace. That's my summer thing anyway."

I glanced over at Red, who nodded, emphatically, then fell asleep. Lou offered me a drink and I accepted, but all Lou had was an opened can of beer and some milk he sniffed and poured down the drain. "I usually refresh myself at the station."

I told him not to worry. "Least I can do is pick up some groceries."

"Lady, don't you know anything about hospitality?"

"I know about paying my own way."

"With your company credit card?"

I reached toward the wall unit full of stereo components. My hands drew circles in the air, searching for a power switch. "What number is your station? I think I like you better on the radio."

Lou grinned. "I'm only on till ten, then my man Tito."

A telephone chirped. Lou answered, "Hey, baby. Can't talk now. I'll catch up with you." He hung up.

I browsed Lou's LP collection. The Beatles, Commodores, Continentals…

The telephone rang again. Lou said, "Hey, baby. I'm kind of tied up right now. I'm workin double shift, filling in for Lila on the evening show."

"How many babies you got?" I asked, after Lou hung up.

"Too many," he said.

I kept thumbing through the sounds—Four Tops, Aretha Franklin, Marvin Gaye, Billy Joel.

"Play anything you like."

"Where's the jazz?"

"Oh, come now. Am I in the company of yet another purist of the pure American art form?"

"I can still get a room."

"Think the hotel's gonna pipe Sonny Rollins in the elevators?"

I pulled down a metal box of 45s in their dog-eared sleeves and handed Lou the third one in the stack.

He smiled. "Brenda Holloway, now you're talking." He snapped a shiny green spindle into the faded Tamala single, spun it on the turntable and danced with himself, closing his eyes, mouthing the pained words as I stood watching and listening. I'm no purist of the pure. I like all kinds of music, in moderation—and jazz in excess. I have always dug Brenda Holloway's voice, the sweet anguish she laid across Barry Gordy's saccharin string arrangements. She opened for the Beatles at Shea Stadium—and might have become another Lady Day if she didn't dump Motown to become housewife to her pastor.

Lou was old enough to remember *Every Little Bit Hurts* when it came out, to fix a time and place in his life to Brenda's soft melancholy. I watched him listening and almost asked where his mind was taking him, but I didn't think I wanted to know him that way.

Red stirred every few beats, his eyes fluttering. I was about to say something to Lou about his musical choice—I mean, here he had complained to me about how depressed his father had always been and then the first record he puts on is Brenda Holloway—but then I remembered that I had picked it. I just reached over and turned down the volume.

"So why exactly are you hangin around with Pops?" Lou asked.

"He told you last night."

"Oh, yeah. Something about tapes."

"One ten-inch reel."

"What's on this reel?"

"Your father's last gig. Monday night at The Sound Box in Baltimore."

Lou was puzzled.

"Lonnie Baylor's Quintet, featuring Felton Payne on tenor, Billy Heron piano, Cole Anderson Bass…*Red Young on drums*?"

"Him I've heard of."

I stood up and walked to the window. Lake Erie was like a sheet of frosted glass. Off in the distance, a thicket of trees piled up against a hillside. A cloud hung over it like smoke.

"You think I got this tape?" Lou asked.

"Your father thinks you might."

"If I did," Lou said, "I don't have it anymore. I sold all that stuff. My father's records, his music. After my divorce."

I turned toward him. "How could you do that?

"He told me that stuff didn't mean a thing to him."

"You really are a bad son."

Lou stood up and flipped the record. I hadn't noticed the side had ended, but now the lyrics I'd only half paid attention to hung in my memory: *I can't take this loneliness you've given me. I can't go on giving my life away*. Lou brought the phono arm down to the groove on Side B and then turned the volume back up. *With a tender love you filled my lonely days. You made me need you darlin' in so many ways.*

"I think I will have that half empty beer," I told him.

Lou got it out of a little fridge beneath the wet bar. He wiped the top of the can with a paper towel and handed it to me.

"I sold all that stuff to a buddy," he said. "A jazz freak like you, you'd probably like Sammy. Walking encyclopedia of jazz. Mr. Cornball Hipster, you know. White guy who just wants to be down, right? I figured he'd appreciate it more than I ever could. I don't have much space over here and you *know* Reyna dumped everything *I* left behind."

I sat with the beer. Almost lowered the music again, but I was starting to like it.

"I think I still have one record," he said, and went thumbing through his albums, pulled out one and showed it to me. *LB Five Sign on the Dotted Line*. A studio set of mainly originals Felton Payne had written while he was upstate on an old drug possession warrant. I'd read the liner notes a hundred times in my mother's garage and studied the jacket cover—a big replica of a safety paper bank check with everyone's name in the top left-hand corner and Emarcy Records as the bank—and I'd listened to those cuts till I could scat every measure.

Did Lou think I was supposed to be impressed that he'd had the good sense not to abandon this one last piece of his own personal musical heritage? I didn't even want to know. "So you think this cat, Sammy, might have the tape?" I asked.

"I don't know, babes."

"My name is Didi."

"Didi," he repeated, and mouthed it a few more times and I half-smiled back at him, mocking his mock.

"Yeah, *Didi,*" I said again.

"Well, I don't remember what it all was I sold him, Didi. We can go see the man when he gets back in town."

"Where is he?"

"Off in Paris or somewhere in France. Jazz festival."

"Montreux?"

"Yeah, that's it."

"Switzerland, not France."

"How come you're not there?" Lou chided. He lifted his father's slouched head off the seat back and propped a sofa cushion behind it.

"When's he getting back?" I asked.

"Don't know," Lou said.

And so it was limbo for the next few weeks, waiting for a guy named Sammy to return from the Swiss Riviera. Heat wave aside, I had myself a relaxing time of it. Lou's bed was comfortable and Lou kept his promise to steer clear of it. He was gone almost half the day, doing the 8 PM to 2 AM show for a vacationing DJ, then his own 2 AM to 8 AM slot (often prerecording the last hour or two so he could get home and sleep). When Lou was in the apartment, he stayed out of my way. Mostly out on the terrace arguing with various women on the phone or sleeping or reading the newspaper, picking up an occasional paperback though he didn't stay with any of them very long. Sometimes he had Anya in the afternoons and would try to keep her busy taking her down to the lake or the indoor skating rink or drawing and coloring at the dining table, but mostly it was a remarkably energized Red hanging out with her when she was over. He'd read her stories or they would make costumes and wear them and pretend to be different creatures. I don't know what kind of father Red had been, but he was a hell of a grandfather. Anya was a sweet child, very energetic and terribly unpredictable. One moment she would be talking staccato nonsense, the next moment she was staring at the face of a clock or the head of a mop gliding across the floor. None of it ever fazed Red. He'd nuzzle against her ear and whisper something and she'd laugh—trance broken, just like that.

A few times I caught Lou watching them, like he felt left out, though he didn't do anything about it. Sometimes he seemed the same way when Red and I would talk late at night. I wanted to say something to Lou about that but didn't think it was my place. One evening Lou was cleaning his fish tank, scooping the colored gravel into a bucket, while Red and I watched a game show. Name that tune was no match for Red Young—he even got *Stardust* on one note—and Lou just stood there looking at us. I told him to sit down but he said he didn't have time. Those neon clowns were temperamental. He had to be quick about disrupting their habitat. After that he had to get to the station. The next morning when I woke up Lou and Red were playing dominos—not saying anything, just gently moving the plastic tiles around, scribbling points on a white pad.

Red took Anya for the whole day on Saturdays and sometimes Sundays: picnic lunch, swimming, bowling, amusement park. I think Lou got a little worried about them and on the second Sunday insisted on going along. He asked me if I wanted to join them. We drove out to Cleveland Stadium for an Indians baseball game and had a blast. This strange little extended family of ours—this unexpected intersection—made me forget the limbo of waiting for Lou's friend to return and the larger limbo in which I found myself. In the hot sun amid the rabid fans, I think Lou felt a similar kind of warmth.

During the last inning, he put his arm around the back of my chair. Then, leaving the stadium, as he grabbed Anya's hand, he also took hold of mine. I let it be. There was something so honest about the gesture—seemed to come straight from his heart. Felt like maybe we really were cousins. And then a moment later it felt like I wouldn't mind if we could somehow be more than that.

But I knew better. Knew anything like that was impossible, more impossible than any of the other impossible relationships I'd had. I mean this one would be doomed from the start. But like Harold Arlen and Johnny Mercer put it: *This time the dream's on me.*

Next morning I wired Nils for another $400 to cover Red's expenses and I let Nils know there would be more charges on the Alamode credit card. Meantime I caught up on some movies, walked residential streets enjoying the family smells of barbecue fires and chlorine. I shopped around for something for my Mom's birthday, coming up next month, something I could send if I wasn't back in New York. I made sure to shower twice a day and get all my clothes clean and forget the funk I'd been living in since I left New York. I thought about digging up a trumpet somewhere—a pawn shop horn or something—to exercise my chops and shatter some air, but I never got around to that.

Lou took Red and Anya and me with him to a 4th of July barbecue at the home of his station manager. There we ate ribs and corn and waited for fireworks in the sky over the lake, then caught televised highlights of the Bicentennial extravaganza from the New York Harbor. Lou hung around me like I might otherwise be lonely or get to like some other dude from his station. It wasn't a problem. Lou had his party mood going and showed that he could actually be a little fun in a goofy sort of way. I thought I could get used to his company, but at the same time, seeing the New York fireworks over the East River, I couldn't help thinking about Derrick. Where was he? Probably on a sidewalk somewhere humming Monk's *Epistrophy* and watching the sky explode in red, white, and blue. Last year we were playing together during the Independence Day fireworks, jamming in a downtown loft for a showing of Polish underground paintings. We did about a twenty minute *Body and Soul*, low and eerie, slow and somber, a neuvo-political reading to the old standard—pretentious as all hell, come to think of it.

The first blast over Lake Erie shook the house and terrified poor Anya. She clutched her ears and spun in tight circles and people looked away, uncomfortably. Red took her inside and gave her a big bowl of candy. Lou watched through a glass door and popped the cap of a fresh beer.

"What are you doing?" I asked him when he offered me the beer. "Go inside!"

"She's fine. I'll just mess it up."

"It doesn't have to be that way," I said. "A girl wants her father."

He looked at me for a moment, took a long sip and carried the beer inside with him. He stood beside his father and eventually put his arm around Anya. She was still pretty freaked out. Hurled her head into Lou's stomach and wouldn't move it from that spot. Lou cradled her and rubbed her back and finally gestured for me to come inside and mouthed, "Let's get out of here."

Anya was still shaking in the backseat of the car as we drove away. Lou took a detour inland, away from the noise and soon she calmed down and fell asleep against her grandfather. Red snored with her while we drove the dark streets of a quiet neighborhood.

"I owe you," Lou whispered to me.

"That's stupid," I said.

"Naw. You shouldn't have had to tell me to go take care of my daughter. But you did, so I owe you. A dinner, at least."

He looked at me, a strong and sober look that scared the crap out of me.

"Did you ever play music?" I asked him. "Did your father ever try to teach you anything?"

"Piano, but I wasn't interested."

A low blast came out of the distance.

"Do you ever wish you had been more interested?"

"Why? So my dad and me could have something else to disagree on?"

"When you play from your soul there's less to disagree on."

"You make it sound so easy."

"I wish it was," I said.

"And don't you worry sometimes," he asked, "that it's not going anywhere? That there's no place else for it to go?"

"There's always somewhere else to go with the music," I said, "if you're willing to keep going." Then I wondered if I hadn't already given up on trying to go there myself.

"I mean that it's already been played," he said. "You know, that cats like our fathers and the cats they played with, that they already sailed all the seas and that all any of the rest of us can do is take folks on a cruise liner over the same waters. You know, like how Mozart and them wrote all the great classical music and it's still great music all these years later."

"I don't know," I said, and really didn't.

"I don't know, either," he said. "Don't know what I'm talking about. Just talking. Who knows about any of it, really? I sure as hell don't, Ms. Didi Heron. I love the records I spin on the radio and like to think I'm helping people get through the late shift at cleaning office buildings and washing soda bottles at the bottling plant and sewing people up at the ER, giving folks a little lift in their can't-sleep lives; but, really, it's all just something to keep people busy between the commercials. In twenty years it'll be background music in the housewares department at Gimbels."

The next morning, Lou got a call from his friend, Sammy. He was back from Europe and invited us all over. Sammy lived in the old business district of Port Clay, in an apartment above a barber shop and shoe repair store. He was a compact dude with a baby face beneath salt and pepper hair. His voice had that tight-mouth Ohio twang I'd been hearing a little too much of during these past weeks.

"Red Young," he said, shaking Red's hand in the doorway. "From the Kenny Clarke school of the modern stick."

"Got that right." Red smiled.

"See, I know more about your dad than you do," Sammy chided Lou.

"You gonna let us in?" Lou sneered.

Sammy got himself out of the way and showed everyone across a thick yellow shag carpet to the scattered pieces of a sectional surrounded by crates of LPs, their withered spines reinforced with scotch tape and covered in plastic. Sammy had a stack of records on the glass brick coffee table. Vintage LB quintet, some big band stuff on obscure labels. "Would you sign them?" Sammy asked Red.

"Surely," Red said. "Got a pen?"

Sammy twisted out the point of his gold Papermate and leaned over to watch Red's signature prance nonchalantly across the album covers. One cover—a trio session of a pianist named Elliott Foy—showed young Red behind a set of drums and a pair of sunglasses, coolly displaying his sticks. His face was full, his cheeks the color that must have inspired his nickname, chin sprouting a goatee.

I shook my head over at Lou, aghast that he could have sold these treasures. "What if Anya wanted them?" I whispered.

"And who are you?" Sammy asked, tipping his head to look at me.

"Didi Heron."

"Any relation to Billy?"

"My father."

"One of the most underrated pianists," he said, and I wanted to hug him. "Your father once did a six-handed session, him and Bud Powell and Billy Strayhorn."

"Tell me about it."

"I don't know details," Sammy said. "Guy at Newport told me about it last year. I have his number. Jazz historian from Madrid by way of Tokyo."

"You don't have to call nobody in Spain or Japan," Red told him. "I know all about them six-handed sessions. Happened at an upstairs joint on the Westside."

"Wasn't it Philly?"

"West Philly," Red told him, "or didn't you know that?"

Sammy smiled uneasily and said, "No, I never knew what part of Philly."

"Me, either," Red told him and laughed. Sammy laughed, and they shook hands. "Think you know it all," Red added. "But you do know a few things, I'll give you that." Red put his arm around Sammy and told Lou, "Yeah, your friend might know a thing or two. More than you!"

None of it seemed to faze Lou, but I felt bad for him. I wanted us to get out of there so I put the question right out there: "You know anything about a tape of their last gig?"

"Last gig?" Sammy asked.

"The LB Quintet. When Lou sold you all these things, were there any reel-to-reel tapes?" I asked.

"You mean original tapes?"

"Me and LB, Felton Payne, and Cole Anderson," Red told him. "Together for the last time."

"And Billy Heron," Sammy added.

Affectionately, he said, "I know who was in the band, chump."

"You're talking original tape, night Lonnie Baylor crashed? Man, that was one of the soaringest reboppin units in the history of jazz!"

"You a smart dude." Red slapped Sammy gently across the cheek.

"If I had that tape I wouldn't be sitting on it. It'd be out on vinyl!"

"Yeah, *real* smart. Where's my cut?" Red chided, digging his finger into Sammy's shoulder.

"Hey, you all oughta do a reunion gig. Get Freddie Hubbard or Art Farmer or Woody Shaw to blow a tribute to LB with you on the drums and—damn, I forgot about your father, Billy. He went down in that accident, too. And my man Cole Anderson."

"*Your* man?" Red laughed.

"I used to catch him sometimes with Booker Ervin at a place in New York. Had a cherrywood bass. Wore a beret that matched it. So how about you and Felton Payne back together? Get Art Farmer, and my man, Barry Harris, maybe Ron Carter on bass. They'd do it to honor LB."

"You crazy?" Red scowled. "Fel been dead for years."

"I know the rumors," Sammy said, "but last I heard Felt Payne was somewhere outside New Haven."

"Last you heard from who?"

"A critic from Barcelona and his boyfriend. Met them at Montreux. Said Felton Payne had played a club in Parkside, Connecticut a few years back."

"Connecticut!" Red laughed. "Now, what would Felton Payne be doin in that state? And if he was alive, don't you think I'd be the first person he'd call?"

Laying in bed that night I was itchy from something in Sammy's apartment—bugs he probably had in that thick shag. My eyes kept snapping open and staring at the vague light streaking against the windows and at thick shadows rushing from the flat white walls into the closet and I kept thinking about Anya, imagining the intense music she might make if she could translate her thoughts to melodic sound.

The next morning, fog drifted in off the lake and seemed to come through the windows and straight into my brain. Nothing keeping me here in Port Clay, Ohio. But no reason to leave, either. I thought maybe Lou would say something when he came in from work, before he went to sleep. I thought the fog might keep him off that terrace. But he just went about his business, like any other morning, and snoozed outside in the mist. Never said anything about it being time for me to move on, nor anything about him wanting me or Red to stay.

It went on like that for days. The morning fog thinned out but the fog of our lives here didn't. It was like a jam session that didn't know when to end, horns trading fours forever, never circling back to the original melody. I kept thinking maybe it was about waiting for Red and Lou to bridge their distance, but there was a quality about them together that made me think this was the only way it was ever going to be. I saw them regarding each other with fondness and even spending time together, quietly being with each other. It was something. It was a lot, and maybe it was enough to keep Red there, even if I didn't stay.

I knew I couldn't. I'd sort of known it all along, but realized for sure when I got a wire from Nils. He wanted an update on things, and something in the beautiful honesty to the temporary life I'd found there in Port Clay made me tell him straight: no tape nowhere and no more ideas. Nothing we could reasonably expect would take us to it.

Nils wired back asking if that was it, if the search was over.

I didn't respond, but I had the feeling he probably wasn't waiting for me to. It was a cool breezy Thursday when that all went down and that night, after Lou had gone to work, I sat down with Red on the low futon sofa like we always did, listening to Lou spin records on the radio and getting to appreciate some of that simple soul music—Ohio Players, BT Express, O'Jays, Donny Hathaway—and like the refrain of that Commodores groove getting a lot of recent play, I told Red it was time for me to move on. I also told him I'd understand if he wanted to stay.

He got all quiet. Seemed about to cry. I looked at him for a minute, then felt like I was intruding and got up and went into another room. When I got there, I was the one crying.

The next evening, Anya came home with Red. They had two bags of groceries and announced that they were cooking dinner. Lou woke up from his siesta and saw them chopping celery and he freaked. Said Anya wasn't old enough to handle a knife, then gave in and said they could cook but started hovering and telling her how to hold the knife and how much oil to put in the pan and where to set the flame, until Anya and Red told him to go away and Lou went back out on the terrace and stared into the setting sun. Then he looked in at me and laughed at himself. I laughed back at him. It was a sweet moment, the kind of moment I might even write a little bebop melody about—a "letter" in my father's parlance—if I thought I had it in me.

The doorbell rang like the first note of that melody I will never write, and Lou came inside to open the door. It was his ex-wife, Anya's mother, Reyna yelling about it not being his night and Red kidnapping Anya from school. Lou was laughing at her temper and that just made it worse. Her voice got louder and Anya came out of the kitchen, screaming and covering her ears with a knife still in one hand and Red right after her saying, "Look what you did."

I thought Reyna might turn and strangle the old man, but the sight of her daughter in pain calmed her right down. Her voice got soft and sweet and she hugged the child, got the knife from her hand and stroked her head till she let go of her ears and all the confusion and terror left her body. "We were making dinner, Mommy," the child said in her clumsy voice. "Are you gonna stay?"

"Not tonight," Reyna said. "It wasn't supposed to be your night here."

"But we're making dinner," Anya said.

Reyna fixed a sullen gaze on Lou and Lou gave it right back to her and in that exchange I thought I might be seeing their whole failed marriage in instant replay. Nothing I really wanted to see, but neither could I make myself turn away. Then Lou glanced at his father for a moment and smiled a far-away smile and told Reyna she could stay, they could all cook dinner together, and before she had a chance to say yes or no, he left his own apartment—just grabbed his keys and slipped on loafers and on his way out the door, he tried to grab me. I swung my arm out of his grasp and he turned around looking so lost that I got up and went with him.

Twenty minutes later, Lou and I were being seated at the restaurant atop the Sheffield Hilton. I hadn't been in a place like it since my high school graduation dinner. Back then Uncle Henry told me I was on a $5 entree budget. That wouldn't have gotten me much on this menu. Lou started ordering up all kinds of stuff—crab cakes and other appetizers—telling me not to feel pressure, just eat as much as I wanted. He got a bottle of wine and did the whole cork-sniffing sip-tasting thing. I said, "Don't you have to be at work soon?" He didn't answer. Just poured me a glass of wine and waited for me to have a sip.

"Ain't it something special?" he asked, and I had to admit it was.

For a while there wasn't anything to say. I think both of us were still preoccupied with what had happened back at the apartment—what a shame it was that Anya could be so fragile, that it took so little to knock her for a loop and mess everything up. Our silence was starting to get to me but nothing I could think of seemed worth saying. So I said the thing I least wanted to say: "I've got to go soon. Back to New York."

Lou sat back in his chair, nodded his head slowly. "Right. I figured, since that tape you're looking for isn't around here."

"But maybe your father will stay on."

"Him? What makes you think I want him to stay?"

"I just think you should. For your daughter, at least."

"Yeah, I should. You got that right."

After steak and shrimp, Lou asked for the desert tray and when I couldn't make up my mind between the mango tart and lemon cheesecake, he ordered me both. The wine was starting to kick in and I was floating lopsided just above my chair.

"You shouldn't do this," I said.

"You gonna tell my daddy on me?"

I liked the mango tart better than the lemon cheesecake but they were both really good. Afterwards, we walked through a narrow park on the lake. There were campfires and swarms of rowdy teenagers. To Lou's delight, they were blasting his station. "Wait till they hear my show tonight," he said. "I'm gonna spin the Lonnie Baylor Quintet."

"You're crazy."

"These kids ought to hear it like that," Lou said. "My dad and your dad, doing it right. Maybe some Miles, too. And Thelonious Monk, John Coltrane. You, too—you got a record I can play? It's their musical heritage. It's the roots of—"

"Who brainwashed you?"

He gave a sly look. "I think you know."

From behind, a voice called out: "Lou." A tall woman jogged toward us in peach-colored sweats and a lot of makeup. She slowed her stride, then ran in place while she ran her mouth: "You were supposed to call me, Lou."

"I've been busy."

The lady nodded, her tongue poking around the inside of her mouth. An uncomfortable stillness stranded the three of us for a moment, then Lou said: "This is Didi. Didi, this is Carole. Carole, the reason I haven't called you back is I've been falling in love with Didi." He took me by the hand, and watched the woman jog off in a daze.

"That wasn't very nice," I said.

"For you or for her?"

"I doubt she ever did anything to deserve that."

Lou smiled. "I don't care about her."

A soft wind blew between us, and when it was gone we were in a kiss, a gentle wintergreen passion that seemed to bring that sweet breeze inside me. A mosquito circled us and we took turns swatting it. Lou came up for air and said, "Damn! I'll *bet* you play a mean trumpet." Then he checked his watch and took my hand and hurried to a payphone to call the station.

"Hey, it's Lou. Get Maxine on. Tell her I need some coverage for a few hours...Gone! She's on tape? *Damn*. I'm gonna be a little late. Run a triple set coming out of her show—*Love Hangover, Get Up and Boogie*—then look on my desk. There's an old jazz album: *LB Five Sign on the Dotted Line*. Play the third cut: *Three Dime*." Then he listened for a moment before saying, "I know it's jazz. I'll explain it on the air. Just play it!"

He hung up and said, "Got to go."

"It's all right," I told him.

"How you feeling?"

"Fine," I told him, and closed my eyes and tried to sort my emotions, which were like a twelve bar solo in a key I couldn't be sure of.

Meanwhile, Lou's voice was saying: "That's good, Didi. That's real good. I feel better than fine."

In the car, he talked about going away for the weekend. A friend of his had a yacht and an island where you could see the Canadian sunset. A lady jock on Lou's station was saying it was eighty degrees. Lou opened his window and inhaled the road's hot breath without flinching. He pulled up to the taxi zone outside his building and ran inside. I ran with him, ran ahead of him. I ran so fast I felt like I might run out of my own body. The elevator stopped me; its slow ascent made me a little dizzy. Lou studied my mood and started to say something but then, approaching his floor, we could already hear the commotion coming from his apartment. The door was open. Reyna was trying to pull Anya out into the hallway. Red was standing in the apartment, all agitated, saying, "Let the girl decide."

"No!" Reyna yelled. "Don't make this about freedom because freedom is something you have and I don't. I'm just trying to take care of this poor child and all your little magic moments ain't making that easier."

"Hey! Hey! Easy, easy…" Lou got between them. He knelt next to Anya and told her, "It's time to go with mommy. That's what time it is."

Red told him, "We just wanted to cook a dinner. Some of that Creole food her grandmother used to make."

It did smell good. Like barbecued mustard.

"Don't be mad at Grandpa!" Anya screamed. For a moment her face seemed to melt like a candle. Then her expression went flat and she gazed up at the spherical light fixture in the hallway ceiling.

"Got that child all twisted," Reyna said. "Turned her against me."

"Reyna!" Lou said. "That's ridiculous."

"The girl doesn't even want to come home."

"This is her home, too."

And then it got ugly for a while, the two of them yelling at the same time—and that got to Red. He put his arm around Anya, squeezed her, then pushed her toward her mother and said, "Never shoulda came here. Never shoulda." He turned to me and said, "Take me back to California. Let's go."

Lou blocked the doorway. "No, Pop, you're staying here with me. Anya can come over whenever she wants."

"It's never been about seeing Anya," Reyna said. "It's only ever been about how long it's gonna last."

"It'll last," Lou said.

"You know I want the best for that child—same as you—but don't get her hopes up if it's not for real."

"It's for real," Lou said, reaching over and pulling Anya toward him.

"And when you get cozy with a woman who doesn't share your fondness for your daughter?" Reyna asked.

"Why you bringing up that shit?"

"Because it's real, Lou. Because I know you."

Lou tried to stare her down but she wouldn't flinch. He looked at me and let out a nervous laugh. Then he ushered me inside the apartment and said, "Don't go."

Truth was, I hadn't thought about leaving *this* soon. I was set to drift for at least a few more days. Just be and let Red be and see what happened, but I guess it was foolish to think it could go on like that or that drifting would lead us anywhere. I think Lou thought I was waiting for him to say something because he got all shaky and said, "All right, you want me to say it? I'll say it. It's not easy, I know you know that, but I will." He cleared his throat and his hand cupped my chin. "You swept me off my feet, lady. Somehow, someway. I got feelings for you. Feelings that are deep and true, like a Brenda Holloway song, like Miles Davis on his muted horn. I'd tell you I love you but I'm afraid that would freak you out and make you run away."

He was right about that. I felt myself starting to run from the moment he spoke his feelings. This did seem the perfect setup. A reason to stay close to Red, and there was some kind of poetic justice to the son of Red Young and the daughter of Billy Heron coming together. Forget the tape. Stop chasing all the stupid dreams. Lou was probably a good husband—though I suppose Reyna might have a different opinion. At least I'd live in style and be treated like a lady—probably, I guess, at least for a while. Lou and I would argue about music, and I would always win. I could play the trumpet for pure enjoyment, could probably find a local spot and be part of the house band. Small scene. Queen bugler of Port Clay. It had its appeal.

"Need a little time to think?" Lou asked.

"No," I said.

"Oh." He looked off—at the tropical fish tank and the shade of jade it momentarily cast at the wall. "You in love with someone back in New York?"

"I'm not sure. I guess maybe I am."

"Who is this guy?"

"Just a musician who's ruined my life and continues to hurt me."

"Sounds like a hell of a guy."

I laughed.

Lou laughed along. "Hey," he said, "no bitterness between us, you understand. You can hang out here if you want. No questions asked."

"I can't," I said, then reached for my duffle.

Lou helped me pack and called a cab, then escorted me back into the living room and toward the front door. I said my goodbyes to everyone, even to Reyna who shook my hand and wished me well. Anya gave me one of her bear hugs and put her teeth on my arm and said, "Later crocodilia." Red put his arm around me and said, "You stay sweet now."

Chapter Nine:

Conjunctive Moonbeams

Sitting in Lou's lobby, catching the light spray from a ceramic fountain behind me, I wondered if I had just made the biggest mistake of my life. One of three elevators opened its doors and seemed to be waiting for me, but I stayed put, thinking about Red and his granddaughter, hoping they would stay together, hoping Lou and Red would keep appreciating each other.

My taxi rolled up outside and the driver blew his horn. The doorman grabbed my duffle and I followed him out of the building. Gnats swirled in the humid air. I swatted my way to the open trunk of the cab, then looked back and saw Red behind me dragging that silly little pink suitcase. "Hey doorman!" he yelled. "Come do your job!"

A few moments later, Red was in the back seat with me. "I'll be back there soon enough," he said. "Lou and Anya. My two crocodilias. But not just yet. Need to get away. Give everyone a minute to think. Lou say I ain't the reason they separated but I don't know. Seemed like that woman and me just don't know how to get along. I wish they would stop treating that child like she ain't right. But I shouldn't always speak on that."

A car pulled up alongside us and hung parallel, flowing with the traffic. Reyna was at the wheel and as she sped ahead, Anya leaned out the passenger window and screamed, "Later, crocodilia!"

I waved to them; Red rolled down his window and shouted back: "Later, crocodilia." Then he snapped his fingers and said, "That's it."

"What's it?"

"The tune I wrote about Lou, back when he was little, nineteen forty-some. What it was called: *Later Crocodilia*. You see, when I would go out to work in the evening, we'd do that thing. You know, say that thing: 'See you later, alligator—in a while, crocodile.' Only Louis always pronounced it crocod*ilia* instead of croco*dile*. Then, one night I said, 'See you later, crocodilia,' and little Lou thought that was the funniest thing anybody ever said. Boy couldn't stop laughin. Then on, every time we'd say goodbye, it was, 'Later, crocodilia.' I wrote a letter about it, like I said. Contrapuntal thing. Beat start in the middle and wouldn't know where was one and where was four. Kind of like fatherhood. Somebody told me Count Basie did a tough arrangement of it couple years ago. *Later Crocodilia*. We played it that night at The Sound Box, matter of fact. Now, I got Anya sayin it too."

Seeing the tiny blur of the train station off in the distance, I asked, "Where exactly are you going now?"

"Was thinkin about goin to check on Felt. Connecticut some place. See if Lou's boy got it right. Got it written down. I don't know if that chump know what he talkin bout but I say let's go see. Already called the information of that town. Parkside. Ain't no Felt Payne with a phone number they know of, but, I just got to be sure. Where you goin?"

"Back to New York, I guess."

"You guess? It ought to matter. Company gives you money and let you take an old man like me half way around the world and help him get back with his son and granddaughter. You ought to be good to that company. When's the next eastbound train?"

"Somewhere, to quote Monk, *Round Midnight*," I told him, and it suddenly hit me that I was going to miss Red terribly.

I leaned over the taxi's partition, asked the driver, "Can you turn on the radio, please? FM, 101.7?"

The driver obliged, and there it was, rattling the speakers: LB and Red and my Daddy along with Felton Payne and Cole Anderson tilting gravity in A-flat on *Three Dimes*. I wanted to hear Lou's on-air explanation to his teenybopper audience, assuming he hadn't been forcibly removed from the microphone, but too soon—barely *two* dimes worth—the cab arrived at the Amtrak station.

Port Clay station was quiet enough to sleep. Until the rumble of an approaching train shook the floor. Our Midnight Cardinal Limited to The Apple. Red hummed the changes to *Three Dimes* as if discovering them for the first time. The train was crowded. Red and I found what seemed the only remaining pair of seats in the last car. No room to stretch out. We sat stiffly next to one another, both staring at the darkness through the window.

My eyes fell closed and then I found myself awakened by the conductor asking for tickets. I paid cash from the small roll I had left. Red thanked me and wiped his eyes on the sleeve of his rumpled shirt.

"You happy or sad?" I asked, when the conductor was gone.

Red kept humming what sounded like a fading memory of LB's solo on *Three Dimes*, then mumbled, "Might not never see him again."

"See who?"

"Carlton. The boy said he'd kill himself when I left. We never really did find a new sound, did we? "

I wanted to disagree and say that what he and Carlton had created was something special, but I didn't think I could fake an ounce of sincerity just then, so I let it go and left him to fall asleep with the echo of his own sad statement, and when his head slumped against my shoulder I didn't have the heart to move it. It was heavier than I would have guessed. I don't know how I managed to fall asleep with the burden of that weight. When I woke up, the train was passing through some industrial wasteland, then ramshackle slum blocks, ghost neighborhoods next to housing projects. Red's eyes were open and reading the grim landscape while pieces of *Three Dimes* still passed through his lips, intermittently. Soon enough we were underneath New York City, and the conductor announced Penn Station.

"I guess this goodbye," Red told me on the platform. He had to get over to Grand Central Station and catch the New Haven Railroad. I had no place in particular to go and said I'd get him on the right subway to Times Square, then east on the IRT 7. Red preferred to walk, wanted to look at New York for a minute. Wasn't much to see, really. Just a lot of streets crowded with people and bags of garbage and neon desperation that seemed to have Red caught between wonder, nostalgia and fear. We got to Grand Central and I kept walking him into the big station, up to the ticket window. I didn't really believe Red would find Felton Payne, but I bought two tickets anyway—one for each of us—hoping that maybe we could dream together a little while longer.

Leaving the city, Red pressed his face against the glass, transfixed. "Harlem," he said. The word put a large rough-edged blob of steam on the window, beyond which stood burnt orange housing projects, tenement rooftops, drying laundry strung like flags above singed lots. "Harlem." Red shook his head with disbelief, then said the word again, this time as a question, then: "I was playin a club on 116th Street. A speakeasy with one-hundred proof gin and whisky and slot machines. They had a house band. Bishop Markel Quartet. I was fillin in on drums for a guy named Ronnie Arch whose girlfriend had cut him right there at the club the night before. Misunderstanding kinda thing. He was in the hospital. Couple nights into that date this kid shows up. Youngster, I mean, seventeen years old. Had a hole in one shoe and his belt seemed to me like someone had weaved it with electric cords. Said he was a horn player from a place called Ottumwa, out in Iowa. Said he just got out of jail. Didn't say why. Said while he was there he met the Bishop, who was there for givin the knife to the gal cut Ronnie Arch. It was some kinda triangular love. But we thinkin this boy just straight crazy. We ain't heard nothin about Bish takin no collar. But when Bishop ain't show up that night, we said, all right, can you blow? Boy took out his ax. It was silver colored. I thought it was made out of tin foil. But it gleamed like the boy had been buffin that baby all day and all night just waitin for a gig.

"Then we stepped out on stage. Piano player—Detroit Scott—said, *Conjunctive Moonbeams,* which was a sorry-ass little nothin tune Bishop had wrote. I watched the kid. How the hell was he supposed to know that tune? Didn't matter. He made up something on the spot that was what *Conjunctive Moonbeams* shoulda always been. Made us follow him. Took a twenty minute solo and had everyone payin attention. Put so much heat into that toy saxophone that I'm tellin you, it started to melt 'round the edges. *Man!*

"Place was robbed that night, middle of the second set—two hoods with thirty-eight pistols—and didn't nobody notice. Afterwards, I talked to the kid. I said I'd try to get him a real horn. Asked him where he learned to blow. Said he'd taught himself."

"What was his name?" I asked.

"Felton Payne."

It was afternoon when we hit Parkside, Connecticut, one stop before New Haven, a suburb of highways and seedling trees, shopping centers beneath sky writers spelling out mortgage rates. The train station was an old barn and we had to hop a cab to Tri-State Rent-a-Car, a pair of wide trailers in a weedy lot next to a freight yard.

At the rental counter was a boy with a helmet of hair above a soft face. His nametag said Andre. I asked him if he knew of Felton Payne, and he replied, suspiciously, "Why you asking me?"

"He's a jazz musician. I'd heard he was playing around here."

"My father's into jazz," Andre said.

"Let's call him," I said.

Andre asked for my driver's license, then handed me a set of Chevrolet keys. I wondered if Alamo had posted security photos of Red and me for not returning the car we'd rented in Ohio. Maybe Lou had returned it for me. I asked Andre for an extra set of keys and handed one to Red. We loaded our bags in the back seat of a blue Nova. Red started the engine.

I asked, "Where we goin?" And Red said he was about to ask me the same question. So we sat in the parking lot, in the wide shadows of a Hellmann's Mayonnaise billboard, and tried to decide. I thumbed through a free newspaper I'd picked up from a rack at the curb. *The Scene* listed three jazz clubs in the area; only The Treble Clef advertised a lunch menu. The drive there took us through woods, over a metal draw bridge, between two factories—one recycled glass, the other made fans. Then past a lake surrounded by houses, then a big concrete fortress called Parkside Plaza Shopping Center.

Parking underground, Red scraped the left fender against a cement column, but still refused to give me the car keys. He got out and looked at the scratches and reached into his back pocket for a hanky and tried to wipe them clean.

The Treble Clef was, according to a lighted mall map, on the top floor, between a linen store and a hot dog stand. Riding the up escalator, I could see Parkside Plaza's ice skating rink down below. Red and I walked passed two jewelry stores, a book store, a candy store and one of those places that sells stuffed animals, cardboard movie star statues, and other expensive crap. Just beyond it was the jazz club, its name in brightly lit purple plastic, surrounded by silhouettes of Miles, Ray Charles, Duke Ellington, and Billie Holiday above a marquee announcing a group called Electric Bop Squad and Next Week: Fender Rhodes Summit.

Inside the place, soft lighting barely illuminated dark walls and fresh flowers did little to brighten the small round tables. On the sound system a piano trio worked a tune one or two tones removed from *How Deep is the Ocean*. The smell of hot grease from the kitchen had me craving a burger so I asked the waiter with his shaggy hair and his Fu Manchu to get me one with bacon and a side of fries. Red was still reading the menu so I took the moment to ask if Felton Payne had played there lately.

The waiter didn't know who I was talking about.

I asked him if the manager was in.

He told me he was the owner!

This shopping mall jazz club was too much for me with its air-conditioned placidness and its sound system which now piped synthesizers doing a bloodless rendition of Strayhorn's *Blood Count*. Red ordered tuna on rye and I asked him if we could take it to go. I called the owner over and handed him the Alamode company Mastercard. A few minutes later he handed me back the card. "I'm afraid," he said, "it didn't go through. Have you got another card?"

I should have expected this—should have realized these were stolen moments. Truth is, I didn't want to imagine that Nils would shut us down.

Chapter Ten:
I Love Paris

I paid cash for the food, dripped ketchup on my burger, and closed back the styrofoam lid. We bought some sodas at a grocery store on the main floor of the mall and went back to the car.

I handed Red pieces of his tuna fish on rye while he drove and I tore through my burger while I read a map and called out directions past long tracts of varnished wooden homes. We took Highway 34 just past the four-leaf clover at the Merritt Parkway to an outdoor strip-mall called Pathmark Plaza. Its twenty stores and their sparkling signs on a brick façade all huddled around a massive Pathmark Food and Drugs. The parking lot was full. Red slowed the car in front of a place called Jazz Fever. A simple black and white sign said: "Swing Nightly, closed Mondays. Featuring the Teddy Yamaguchi Nine Piece All-Stars."

Red double parked while I got out.

Jazz Fever's door was locked, but I kept pounding on it while sun pounded my shoulders and finally the door crept open. An elderly woman poked out her head. Her skin was the texture of parchment, her hair in a silver bun.

"I'm looking for Felton Payne," I told her

"Haven't seen him around," the woman said.

"Then you know him?" I asked.

"Tenor man supreme. To the bone."

"Do you know where he is?"

"Not really," she said.

"Do you know where he might be?"

"Couldn't tell you, not exactly."

"Is he alive?" I asked.

"No idea."

"When did you last see him?"

"Wish I could say. He your relative?"

"Yeah, we're related. Have you seen him recently? I mean, in the last few days, weeks? Was he living around here?"

"That's what I heard. But I never seen him. I was in the hospital, you see. Had a pin stuck in my hip. Helps me to walk. Wasn't myself for a while. I'm starting to feel better though."

"Who runs this club?"

"I do."

"Who ran it while you were in the hospital?"

"We closed."

I thanked her and got back into the car. Unsure where else to go or what else to do, I let Red steer into another outdoor mall, a large new one, featuring a hardware emporium and garden shop. Red drove along the edge of the parking lot, and I read storefronts—some open for business, others promising a grand opening. A bookstore, an insulation and pool supply. A little further down was PJ's Records.

"Maybe they know something in there," I said, hopping out as soon as Red stopped.

Inside was chilly and swarming with the sound of repeating tonic triads and a pounding 4/4. I thought I recognized one of the teenagers working behind the counter. "Andre?"

"Do I know you?" he asked. He was taller than he'd seemed behind the rent-a-car counter and the neon green PJ Records shirt brought out his eyes. "I don't suppose you'd know if there was a jazz club around here."

"Think 'cause I'm black I gotta know jazz?"

"You should," I told him, then backed up and said I was sorry, which seemed to soften him. He told me it was all right and then asked if there was anything else he might be able to help me with.

"Come on with me a moment," I said and he followed me toward the jazz aisle. My eyes jumped from Cannonball Adderly to Charlie Parker, then back to Payne, Felton Payne. I grabbed the *Payne Memorial Album*. It showed Felton in a restive pose, his ax on his lap, his mind in some far away land, his shirt collar drooping, sweat-soaked. I held it out to the young man. "That's him," I said. "That's Felton Payne. The cat we're looking for."

Andre studied the photo, nodding. He seemed to appreciate the little jazz lesson. "Sorry I can't help you," he said, "but anyway, doesn't *memorial* album mean the person's dead?"

"Usually, yeah," I said. "But maybe not always."

Back in the car, I told Red, "Let's get out of here. I'm going home."

Red sat still for a while, wouldn't talk.

"Come on," I said. "Lou wants you with him and so does Anya. That's what matters."

"But if my man...If Felt out here somewhere...Got to be sure. I know *I'm* alive and I know if Felton's alive he probably thinks I'm dead." Red closed his eyes and breathed through his nose, then rolled down the window and spit. He shook his head and rolled the window back up, seeming tired from the effort. "All right, then. Let's just go. Forget the whole thing and let's go. Let's get a ice cream and then get goin."

On the other side of the hardware emporium was 31 Flavors, cold and bright and crowded. I took a number and we waited, not long. Red had two scoops of pistachio on a sugar cone. I had a single scoop of something called fudge ripple. I broke my last $100 bill and I folded the change into my wallet and dropped it in my purse, then zipped it up. An arm landed on the back of my neck and I turned to see who it was and felt my purse strap tear away from my shoulder. I spun around. A shirtless man—pimply back and Levis—was already through the front door, running in bare feet.

"Hey!" I shrieked. "Hey! Stop him!" But everyone around me was as frozen as the ice cream in its drums. "My purse!"

I dropped my cone and ran to the door and kept going.

The guy with my purse dodged a row of cars, his legs kicking high as he ran. My strides were longer, more efficient. I took a low shrub like a track hurdle—but this guy was fast. He cut between the hardware store entrance and its garden shop, toward a delivery truck parked at a loading dock. He ducked under the rear gate, then vaulted into a row of bushes.

Some men on the loading dock cheered as I ran by.

"Why don't you do something?" I yelled at them.

They laughed and continued to applaud.

I did the limbo beneath the truck gate and fell sideways, skidding on both knees, then sprang back to my feet stepping faster with that pain propulsion. I jumped down through the bushes and found myself on fresh black tar, my chin and one arm bleeding slightly. Headlights, a grill—a car! A loud honk sent me into a bank of ivy. I got my bearings. I had just crossed a highway onramp, was on the shoulder of the Merritt Parkway. I couldn't see the guy with my purse anymore. I noticed a narrow trail leading down below the highway. I followed the ivy, a curving descent into a foul nitrogen odor, grumbling noises getting louder, mostly talk, some music, an encampment, a shantytown of scrap wood and aluminum and cardboard. People stood and sat around, some in rags, some in casual clothes, one man in a three piece suit about two sizes too small. There was a pair of long bedraggled church benches, a big table made of telephone cable spools, a rotting set of bleachers upon which sat a man and a woman, huddled under a blanket. No one noticed me. Music, strangely gasping music kept coming from somewhere. My eyes searched around for the source—and I saw my purse. It was at the top of a pile of garbage. I grabbed it. The credit card was still there. So was the dental floss, hand-wipes, and Red's return train ticket. Missing was my lipstick, a roll of fruity Certs, and the cash.

I used a hand-wipe on my face and neck and hands and moved across the trash and weeds toward the strange assortment of human forms. Some really heavy vehicle passed overhead and made the ground beneath us shiver.

"Anybody seen the motherfucker who stole my money?" I asked.

Vacant stares answered. A large man in a boxer's robe asked, "You looking to get in here?"

"I'm looking for my money!" I said. The music had stopped momentarily.

"We're afraid," said the man in the boxer's robe, "that the gentleman who ran through here with your funds had some other destination in mind."

"Must be," someone else said.

The robed man had a cigar that he twirled with his fingers. "Don't usually take on newcomers, but in your case, if you can come up with the hundred dollar membership fee..."

I wasn't at all sure what was going on, but something inside me almost could imagine dropping out of life right here right now. Disappear under the Merritt Parkway.

The music started up again. It came from a weary saxophone somewhere, started in the middle of a musical phrase and gyrated crazily around the same melodic pattern in alternating directions. It might have been a variation of *I Love Paris* in 4/4 in revolving keys marinated in funk with snatches of *Tobacco Road* and *Brother Can You Spare A Dime?*

"Say," someone said, "you gonna report it to the police?"

But my attention was on the music. Seemed like it was coming from behind the bleachers. I moved in that direction, and saw, between the rotting boards, the back of a head knotted with brown hair and the long sensuous neck of a tenor sax.

"Who's that over there?" I asked.

"You mean old boy with the saxophone?" someone asked.

"Who is he?" I asked.

"He don't have a name. Lived here before we did. Got his own little shack behind that post. Keeps to himself. Doesn't got any money. Doesn't want any. We give him food is all he wants. Food and coffee and Pepsi Cola with extra sugar in it."

The man in the three piece suit laid a pair of reading glasses across his nose, then got close to me and added, "He told me he doesn't want money because he'll use it on heroin. Just wants food. He don't bother no one. He ain't steal your money."

I walked around the bleachers, stood behind them. The tenor player smelled of coffee grounds and the heavy sour aroma of saxophone cork grease. Notes wheezed out of his horn, then twisted into a rant, then a howl. I watched for a long while and noticed that his playing seemed to change direction with the flow of traffic. I kept staring. Got closer and saw his soft features. His very dark eyes rolled and darted as he played. I hadn't seen Felton Payne in person since I was four years old and photos are never quite like the people they represent, and to me he had the kind of face that never quite looked the same way twice.

I walked around him, so that he would notice me, but he kept turning his back. He finished a lick and jerked the sax from his mouth. It was a lusterless horn, the reed fused to the cork with black electrician's tape. He kept turning himself away from me and said nothing.

"Felton?" I asked, and got no response. "Felton Payne?"

He spun round and stared at me, then blew *Star Eyes* slow and breathy, then choppy, then he let the reed slide out of his mouth. "You my last living fan?" he croaked slowly.

I smiled.

"You wanna get a motel room?"

"I want to take you to meet a friend."

"She look like you?"

"He looks more like you: Red Young."

Felton slid the reed into his mouth and played a far away D-flat, which became the first soft tone of a very slow, off-tempo, *All God's Chillun Got Rhythm*. Then, without removing the instrument from his mouth, Felton said, "Red Young."

"Yes, Red Young."

"One, two, three, four," Felton mumbled. "Uno, dos, tres, quatro."

I wondered if the man was crazy—or dangerous. But I wasn't about to leave him there. "Red's waiting."

"Red Young?" Felton asked, the reed slipping from his jaws.

"Yes."

Felton shook his head. "Red Young is dead."

"According to who?"

"Time, baby. According to time."

"So are you, according to time and the *Jazz Encyclopedia*."

"Maybe we're all in heaven," he said with a sweeping gesture.

"We're definitely not in heaven," I said.

"How you know that, lady?"

"'Cause my father's not here."

"*Your* father…Who art in Heaven?"

"My father, Billy Heron."

Felton laughed. "You're Billy Heron's kid and you got Red Young and now you want me?"

"That's right."

Felton tucked his instrument under his arm and walked to his shack, which looked like a large dog house nailed together with rotting boards. From inside of it he rolled out a shopping cart overflowing with clothes and hardened canvas bags. Felton laid his ax on top. "Don't trust these people," he wheezed, and steered the cart over the rough ground toward the bushes that led back up to the world.

Felton's wheezing echoed as we moved. He maneuvered the shopping cart with an expertise that was impressive as it was sad, up and down curbs, across the freeway onramp and into the back of the shopping center.

I wanted to tell him how excited I was, how I'd come up hearing him as the definitive tenor sax player in my life, but I didn't think he would be interested, so I kept quiet. We passed the loading dock. Three men were still there. They applauded me and yelled their congratulations. One said something about bringing a thief to justice. Felton and I paid no mind. I got out in front of him and grabbed the front of the shopping cart and pulled as together we climbed the slight incline into the parking lot.

I glanced toward 31 Flavors. Red stood outside, all worried. He didn't see Felton and me at first. I watched Felton for a moment. He tried to hold in the wheezing and wound up spitting blood, as we approached the curb.

Red backed away from the man with the shopping cart, then looked at me, as if for protection. "Hey man," Red muttered, and then his lips went limp his head tilted way back, and his eyes sank so that it almost appeared that he was wearing sunglasses. He said, weakly, "No."

Felton stopped his cart and pivoted toward me. "You tryin to tell me that's Red Young?"

The two men were parking spaces apart, neither making a move toward the other. "Fuck makes you think I want to see Red Young?" Felton asked.

I got between them. "Hey!"

"Red Young's a punk-ass! Dropped out the scene. Left me flat."

"Don't you talk that way to my friend," I said, and thought we might have to fight.

But Red explained: "That's just Felton. Boy don't know how to be sad."

"You old dried up raisin," Felton said, and Red crept toward him, reaching out with his hand. Both men seemed reluctant to touch what they weren't sure was real.

Finally, Felton slapped Red's extended palm, then held on, pulled Red to him. Red clutched on to Felton at the shoulders. Felton reached around Red and the two men stood still in each other's arms.

Then they sat next to each other on the curb and Felton apologized for the things he'd just said and for smelling bad, and Red said he didn't know what Felt was talking about. They got caught up. Felton's words came slowly. He couldn't remember exactly what year the club dates had stopped happening or when the drug habit had gotten out of control or when it had gotten back under control or when it stopped mattering to him where he lived or whether it had ever really stopped mattering. Red didn't get specific about what he'd been doing for the past twenty years. The two men tried to figure out when they'd last seen each other. Was it really LB's funeral? Red pulled out his wallet and showed his old friend photos of Lou and Anya. Felton asked if we could get something to eat.

The stable mates walked arm in arm with me behind them pushing Felton's cart and looking around for the car. Passing PJ's Records, I couldn't resist: "Felton, you gotta come in here for a minute."

"I don't go in them places."

"Just for a minute," I said, and he let me steer him and his cart inside and down to the jazz aisle. I grabbed up his *Memorial Album*, and showed it to him. Felton looked it over, the photo of his long ago self, and smirked at the worried expression on his youthful face. Then he read the tune selection on the back. "*Incidental Afternoon*! I was tired and all strung out when I blew that. Didn't put *no* fire in it. And they left off *Happy Go Lucky*."

I spotted my friend, Andre. He was across the store hanging a Bootsy Collins poster on the wall. I hollered his name and he looked up. "You got a pen?" I yelled.

Before Andre could answer, a young guy with sweaty hair and a feather duster in his back pocket was in my face. His badge said Mike Diatello, Manager. "Excuse me," he said, nodding toward Felton. "I want him and his shopping cart out of my store!"

I jabbed Mike Diatello with the plastic corner of the *Felton Payne Memorial Album*, then waved the cover in front of him.

"Felton Payne, man. He's a great American musician. He's alive. He's in your store!"

"It's all right," Felton wheezed. "Let's go."

"They can sell your album but you can't come in?"

Mike Diatello snapped his fingers over at Andre and told him to call the police.

My determined stare froze Andre.

Diatello snapped his finger again and said, "What's the problem?"

"Nothing," Felton Payne answered. "I'm leaving." He took the reins of his cart, then grabbed me and dragged me toward the door.

His strength surprised me—for a moment—and then it was gone and I was holding him up. We were at the store entrance, next to a counter full of marijuana pipes and roach clips. Felton's gasps got slower, longer and knotted up like he was sucking cement through a straw. I fell backwards to catch his fall, and we rolled to the floor together. A moment later Red was kneeling next to us, asking, "What happened?"

"I don't know!" I told him.

"Get him out of here!" Mike Diatello was yelling. He pushed Felton's shopping cart onto the sidewalk and let it fall and spill Felt's saxophone and the top layer of his possessions. Customers crowded around us. And then on the store stereo system, suddenly: the unmistakable sound of Felton Payne, from his memorial album, an off-minor thing called *Oven Mitt*.

I got up and screamed, "Call an ambulance! Somebody call an ambulance!" Then I saw Andre behind the counter, next to the stereo controls, *Felton Payne Memorial Album* jacket in hand, ear to the phone, talking urgently.

Chapter Eleven:

Now's the Time

Two paramedics pulled Felton onto a stretcher and picked him off the floor. One asked him how he felt while the other to his chest. They let Red ride along to the hospital. I went for the car to follow but on the way saw someone at the garbage dumpster behind a convenience store, emptying Felton Payne's shopping cart.

"Hey!" I ran. "Hey, stop!"

The girl squinted. She wore a brown Key Food vest, her hair knotted in a rubber band. Her name tag said Karen.

"That cart belongs to someone."

"Relax, lady. This cart belongs to Key Food. Check it out." She pointed to the light red placard with the Key Food emblem.

"I'm sorry," I said. "But please. My friend...Let me empty it. Then you can have the cart. Just give me a minute."

She told me to hurry up.

I brought the car over and she helped me load up: shoes, pants, shirts, a duffle bag, a book of Amiri Baraka poetry, a shoe box of tools. Warm drizzle started to fall.

I thanked Karen. Might have given her some money if I hadn't just been robbed. Karen said, "It's all right, lady. You take care of yourself, huh?" Then she hoisted the empty shopping cart onto the back of a pickup truck.

I leaned my head over the rim of the dumpster to see what of Felton's had already been tossed. At the top of the pile: his saxophone, the reed now dangling from its cork by a strip of tape. I was glad I hadn't given Karen a tip.

I grabbed the rusting edge of the dumpster, hoisted myself up and dove in, breathing slowly through my mouth. I lifted the sax, wiped the reed and mouthpiece on my sleeve. I fingered the buttons, then probed the dents on the neck. I tucked the instrument under my arm and dug deeper in the heavy stench of the dumpster. I found a trenchcoat and hat and wondered if they belonged to Felton. I checked the pockets of the coat for something that might let me know. The pockets were huge, like pillow cases. Inside one was a pair of sunglasses. Inside the other, a box. A flat ten-inch box.

The warm drizzle kept falling and I raised my head toward those reluctant rain clouds, then put the musty trenchcoat over my head, like a tent. I leaned sideways, enough to let in some light, and examined the box. It said Scotch Brand 3M recording tape in light brown letters. Tattered edges within a heavy plastic wrapper. I read the tight brown letters printed vertically along the spine: *LB Quintet at The Sound Box*.

On the sinking surface of that garbage, my unsteady feet made me question the actuality of the discovery.

I slid the flat box back in the pocket, then put the coat on. It was heavy with sweat and time. I picked up the sax and my fingers probed all the tiny dents along its long neck. I twisted out the reed and the cork then put them, along with a few other odd items, in the other big coat pocket. I clutched the instrument under my arm while I scaled up and over the ledge of the dumpster and came down on the reassuring, hard pavement. I brushed the filth from my hair and hands, and got into the rented car.

I just sat there for a long time with the strong odor of Felton Payne's degradation—checking myself. I took that flat box out of the raincoat pocket and looked at it, at the lettering. *LB Quintet at The Sound Box*. I drove to a phone booth and flipped through the yellow pages. Ranges and Ovens,

Refrigeration, Real Estate, Record Stores, Recording—a studio in New Haven. I called up and got a guy named Glen, and I was about to give him a bullshit story about scouting new facilities for GLX Music to use outside New York City, but with Felton on the way to the hospital, I felt a child's kind of superstition. So I told the truth and Glen said, all right, but hurry up before they closed. Ten minutes later, I was in an air-conditioned sound booth with my tape, an Ampex machine and a pair of headphones clamped on my ears. My fingernails were all chipped and broken, but my pinky nail had enough edge to break the crude masking tape seal around the box to get it open. The reel was gray metal, dull and smooth. The tape itself gleamed chocolate brown. Gently, I removed it from the box, picked at the white leader until it came loose, then I threaded it up. I sat back in the swiveling chair. A clock on the pegboard wall said 4:55. But time of day had never been so irrelevant to me. The pegboard sagged with sheets of cueing codes, telephone numbers, and pizza delivery coupons.

I gripped the play lever and twisted it and waited. At first, I didn't hear anything but the clicking whir of the air-conditioner from somewhere above my head. Then came a faint hiss, then static, then a vague scratching sound—which I imagined, hopefully, were dishes in The Sound Box kitchen—and then a hard sucking, like a chorus of cigarette smokers, which gave way to more static, then a fuzzy voice which faded in and out, like this:

"...elcome...Sound...ox...name...Harry...sdale, but the boys...all me Rags..." I cringed at the man's patronizing voice. "...Introduce...cats...forefront of jazz today...Drummer, Red...ist, Cole Ander...e-anist, Billy He...owes me...dollars... poker last night. Ha ha! The incomp...Felto...saxo...And the liv...gend...trumpet, my man...Baylor! Put...hands toge... Lonnie Bay...quintet!"

I could make out mildly enthusiastic applause, then bits and pieces of a piano and sax conversation—my daddy and Felton—joined by drums smashing in, then fading in and out. It was *Morningside Drive*—at a high-paced tempo—and

I guess I know that tune so intimately that my mind was able to fill in what had dropped out. I couldn't hear LB's horn at all and I was afraid it had vanished altogether from the magnetic track. I concentrated on my father's smooth comping, which was quite unspectacular and made me wonder if maybe that was all it would be. People say things, things to make other people happy, especially a daughter looking for the sound of her father. Maybe no one ever thought I'd find this damn tape anyway.

But I kept on listening.

Then, without warning—after a very long pause—the trumpet of Lonnie Baylor joined the spasmodic melodic fracas. I made out a single long hollow B-flat into the tunnel of sound. I kept filling in the sound gaps and after a while couldn't distinguish what was coming through those headphones and what was my own musical instinct, memory, and imagination. Lonnie's B-flat dropped an octave and burrowed way down into the lower register, carrying me back into the memories Red had given me. Even if Billy Heron wasn't spectacular on that night, he played the chords beneath something that promised, as always, to be a transformation in sound. And this was Billy's tune, his statement.

I closed my eyes and constructed The Sound Box in my imagination. Could see the notes flying out of LB's horn as he took his solo. Colored smoke. A rainbow of sound. Felton soloed simultaneously, cacophonically. I listened for the heartbeat, heard Red keeping time, tapping the traps, rolling over the snare, laying some rhythmic suspension between the bars. Dad played a four-bar interlude and brought the tune way down into an upbeat lullaby and took a solo, and in that solo—just as Stan Man and Red had promised—Billy broke out, he came on. There it was, coming into me and through me, and I kept my eyes shut and could see his hands dancing across the octaves. Then the horns swung in.

Morningside Drive wound round the bend, but the heartbeat continued through the applause and launched into muted double-time. A wild chord pattern, explosive horn interplay, monster comping from the piano. I kicked way back in my chair and let the music become my central nervous system. Heard the changes to *You've Changed*. Then *Darn That Dream* in jumping two-note phrases. I closed my eyes and for a moment thought I could smell the mixture of Dad's aftershave and the butterscotch on his breath. The fourth tune was something I'd never heard before and wanted to somehow identify. I sprang open my eyes, moved to the beat. I picked up the empty tape box and examined it. Inside was a piece of thin cardboard. A long rectangle, about two inches by six. It stuck to the bottom of the box. A hand scrawled list of tunes. On it said:

The Lineup: 1st Set
1: Morningside Drive
2: You've Changed
3: Darn That Dream
4: That 6/4 Feeling
5: The Heartbeat
6: Spontaneous Combustion
7: How High the Blue Moon
8: Later Crocodilia

Set Two
9: Conjunctive Moonbeams
10: I Love Paris
11: Now's The Time
12: Embraceable Spirit
13: That Lonnie Baylor Sound
14: Morningside Drive

That 6/4 Feeling was still going in the headphones, a semi-waltzing pattern. I closed my eyes again and returned to The Sound Box. Could hear the applause grow a little louder with each tune. *The Heartbeat*, next up, was an eight minute drum splash with piano and horn riding just beneath the wave. Then *Spontaneous Combustion* erupted with volcanic polytones, Billy Heron all over it. *How High The Blue Moon* was something else—finger poppin' soul to the core. *Later Crocodilia* was that get happy, sweet set of chromatic changes. Just the thing to put a grown woman back onto her daddy's lap.

Then the music stopped and I listened, still filling in the gaps, to Lonnie Baylor's introductions: "To my right, my right hand man on the tenor, Felton Payne…Behind me, on bass, the incomparable Cole Anderson…Next to him, my drummer, my heartbeat, Mr. Josh 'Red' Young…And to my left, on the piano…" The applause was heavy and started even before the name was spoken: "Let me put it this way, y'all: this is now the Billy Heron Quintet with Lonnie Baylor!" And Lonnie laughed and laughed through the applause, then promised to come back for another set.

I consulted the second set list. *Conjunctive Moonbeams*, the tune that, according to Red, Felton Payne reinvented with a tin saxophone in Harlem: three-bar chaos two-stepping toward four-part harmony. I wondered whose back-slanted handwriting had written the names of the tunes. I flipped the card and saw the other side: two faded tickets of some kind, perforated together. They were gray, probably had once been green or maybe blue. They said, "Pennsylvania Railroad." Handwritten names and destination:

Lonnie Baylor
Baltimore to Boston

Billy Heron
Baltimore to Boston

"Damn," I said, aloud. Stan Duboclet—that son-of-a-bitch. Too damn stupid or high to notice he was writing the sets on the backs of two train tickets that were two men's tickets to the rest of their lives. If there is a jazz heaven, as Red had told his sis, then, yeah, Dad and LB are surely there. And if there is a jazz hell, I say that's where Stan Man has got to go.

I Love Paris came over my headphones. With an uptempo, funky beat it was almost unrecognizable. Next was *Now's The Time*, tribute to the Bird, played with a burning rage to the heartbeat and a determined punctuality in my Dad's hammered-in colorations.

I kept waiting for the last tune, the reprise of *Morningside Drive*, which I imagined was in honor of my father and the way he had flexed it hard for the folks in the club that night, but as the reel spun on, to my horror, the sound images disappeared altogether and I could no longer fill in the missing tones. I felt a hunger that was all up and down my arms and the back of my neck and it filled me with something like dread but more like rage. I thought this must be what the dope addict feels like when he needs a fix.

I turned the knob from play to stop and went out into the hallway and found a guy in an alcove, leaning on a refrigerator, trimming his beard into a trash can, and watching a TV dinner in a toaster oven. I asked for his help and he took a whiff of me and that coat and gave me a look, but then introduced himself as Ralph and brought his ravioli with him back to the sound room.

He eased the headphones over his ears and pushed play. His face tightened. He pulled on his beard, listening.

"What is this?" he asked.

"It's a legendary performance from 1956. Can it be restored? Do you know?"

Ralph listened some more, then rewound the tape for a while and listened again, eyes closed. I wished there was a way for me to convey what I had heard before, the enchantment of my imaginings. Ralph pulled off the headphones and looked past me.

"Nothing?" I asked.

"It's gone," Ralph said, and pulled the headphones out of their jack so that the music emerged from the tape player's loudspeaker. Hearing it along with Ralph, I knew how faded out it really was and how much I had filled in: practically all of it. A strangled tone every two or three beats, surrounded by the most horrible silence.

Chapter Twelve:

Embraceable Spirit

There were only two hospitals in the area. St. Joseph's Memorial and Peat Swamp Public Health Center. We all know which one a homeless guy gets delivered to, so I headed out Swamp Road a few miles, then into the metered lot adjacent to a cinder block building with tiny barred windows.

Inside the waiting area, people were crammed into plastic chairs and moving tentatively between hard walls. A pale man held his chest and leaned against a counter, a pregnant woman tried to entertain two small children with a huge cardboard book. I carried myself past all that, still wearing Felton's musty raincoat, sweating beneath it—my funk harmonizing with his funk—and made it to the Priority Needs Section, a crowded hall of barely conscious people. A pair of medical workers were too busy to accost me. Red was sitting on the edge of a small cot, hovering over Felton, who was propped against a monitor, tubes all in his arms and nose.

Red was happy to see me. "Felt's got some good news," he said.

"The good news is that he's still alive," said a voice behind us. A young doctor with messy hair and smudged bifocals.

Felton coughed out the words, "Y'all better wait outside."

Red and I started to go, but the doctor said: "If you're his friends, you should hear this. I'm Doctor Kaufman. Me and Felton go back. Ain't that right, bro?"

Felton nodded in the affirmative.

"Raise Up Rehab in New Haven," the doctor said. "I told him then and I'm gonna tell him and you all now. He needs a new instrument."

"Go on, man," Felton said. "Leave that shit alone."

"Musta been two years ago, hey, Felton? I told you to quit smoking."

"I did."

"And quit blowing a sax with a hole in it, or you would get a hole in your lung?"

"New ax cost big money," Felton wheezed.

"Then you should have stopped playing."

"Giving up the cigarettes. That was easy, relatively speaking."

Dr. Kaufman had his pen out, was scribbling something. Said, "Here's your prescription, man," and handed it to Felton.

It was a check. "Five hundred dollars!" Felton said.

"Is that enough?" the doctor asked.

"That's beautiful, man. I can't accept it."

But Dr. Kaufman wouldn't take it back. He said, "I'm gonna get you some Medicaid money and some oxygen, that's all you really need. Then I gotta turn you loose."

And he moved on to another patient.

Felton stared at the check, shaking his head.

"I wasn't crazy," Red mumbled. "You're dad and me and Felt and Cole with Lonnie at The Sound Box. I gave that tape to Felt to hold after the funeral. And that's the last we saw each other. But he had it all along."

"Only now I ain't got it," Felt's voice creaked out. "Ain't got a damn thing."

I told him I had his stuff in the car and he looked up, saw his coat.

"Tape right there in the right pocket," he said.

I turned away and faced the far window, which looked onto a dark hallway.

"What's a matter?" Red asked.

"I already listened. It's all faded out."

Felton tightened his face at me, accusingly. Red let his head hang, then picked it up. "You thread that shit up right?" Felton asked.

"Yes," I said.

"Did you thread it through the heads?" Red asked.

"Maybe the tape player was broke," Felton added.

"I took it to a studio in New Haven. They know what they're doing."

Red wasn't having it. Felton either. He had me find Dr. Kaufman and asked if there was any way we could get a reel-to-reel tape player in there. Dr. Kaufman made a few phone calls and within an hour a colleague of his arrived with a Teac 1000. We threaded The Sound Box tape: still inaudible. Then we all sat there, just dazed with our collective disappointment. I asked Felton when was the last time he had listened to it.

"Never did," he replied.

"All those years?" Red asked.

"Yeah," was Felton's answer. "Tough years."

"You never listened."

"Never opened the box."

"There you go," Red said.

"Just too sad," Felton said, and Red added: "Amen." Then told me, "Don't cry."

"I'm not crying," I said, and realized that I was.

"You were gonna make a lotta money off that tape, weren't you?" Felton asked me, in the strained whisper that was his voice.

"Ain't about the money," Red told him. "She ain't in this for no coins. She in it for the music, for Billy. Billy, man, he played good that night. Played real good."

"I know it," Felt said, and now he had tears welling up. "I'm sorry about this. Very sorry. That I held it—held it while you were out there needing to hear it."

"Don't feel bad," I told him. "It's just one of those things."

A dude in a gray coat rolled an oxygen tank next to Felton and plugged his tube into it. Red and I watched him breathe easy for a while, until a lady with cracked reading glasses hanging off her neck came by and handed Felt his discharge papers. Felt glanced faintly toward a blank wall at the other end of the room. I didn't say anything to him. Was afraid to—but then I told him to come on, follow me—him and Red—and when we got outside I saw a sign for a motel across the street. The sign said "MuTEL" with its partially burned out "o." They had rooms for us—with numbers that didn't make sense for such a small place, room 335 downstairs with two twins and 608 upstairs in the back with a queen—and the cat at the front desk didn't bother to call in my company credit card. I took Red and Felton to their room and stayed there a minute to watch them get situated. Felt found places to put his stuff and picked out the bed that was next to the window. He went in the bathroom and turned on the shower. He wasn't bashful—came out drying himself with a towel while his clothes, which he'd washed along with his body, hung drying on all the towel racks and above the shower curtain.

I thought I should go before I saw more than I'd ever want to. I kissed Red on the side of his face. Wanted him to know, without having to say it, how glad I was that I'd gotten to know him and that I'd helped him find Felton. For me, right then, that was more important than any music on any tape.

Alone in room 608 I tried to stay philosophical. Respect and recognition from the crowd matters less than the love and memory of the individual heart, doesn't it? So if I was the only living soul who ever got to hear what was on that tape—such as I had—that was solid. I turned off the lights in the room and let that idea fill up the darkness. I pulled the bed covers up over my head and kicked off my pants and gave in to the sweet paralysis of sleep. I was deep in a dream when Red's faint voice reached in and for a while I refused to let it wake me up—just incorporated the sound into my floating spinning nothing. But the funk in deep freeze of the two old men, breath and bodies all together, opened my eyes.

"You're gonna get your tape," Red told me. "Gonna do it, Didi. Gonna re-record it."

"How'd you get in here?" I asked him, but Red didn't seem to hear me. His eyes were bugging out.

"Felton got money for a new ax," he said.

Felt was behind him, nodding *yeah!* And kept nodding through Red's whole statement. "And that boy remembers what we played that night, every note. My memory startin to work, too. Me and Felt, we know those cuts. Know that interplay rather so intimately."

"You're crazy," I told him.

"I can dominate the toms now, Didi. You have surely messed up my agony."

"Felt can barely breathe!"

"Boy got ways to make a lotta sound out of a little."

I won't lie—I dug their enthusiasm. Crazy as it sounded, I didn't want to mess with their nutty rapture, so I avoided the unanswerable question. Instead I asked: "Who are you gonna get to play bass?"

Red thought it through. "Cole was a workman. His sound's not hard to come by. I got a good mind to call my boy Carlton. I had been showin him how to walk that sucker, how to swing—like Mingus and Blanton."

"What about piano?" I asked, knowing the answer, but not wanting to know.

"We'll find somebody."

It took all of the next morning to get Felton's check cashed and find Lalo's Music in New Haven. They only had a few second-hand tenors and Felt knew right away it was going to be the Giardinelli with a soft-medium La Voz reed. Seeing it, Felt gave a chipped-tooth smile and reached out his arms, waiting to have it handed to him. He fingered the low F and high F-sharp keys tentatively, took a long drag on his oxygen tube, blew the instrument into the altissimo register, and did some one-handed multi-phonics. The horn had some deep scratches and the case must have been chewed by an animal, but there were no holes in the brass and the price was $175.

Red put money down on a not-too-shabby set of Pearls with $25 weekly payments. The sticks Red had to buy outright. He tested the kit in the shop, did some *Klook Kloppin,* and raised some eyebrows on the young faces.

In the subsequent three-way quiet, a question hung. *The* very large and unanswerable question. I wasn't about to ask. But the question kept hanging there until Felton asked, "You think Art would be game?"

"Art Farmer?" Red asked.

"He still around, ain't he?"

"Guess so."

"You think he'd help us out?" Felton asked.

"I don't know, Felt." Red rubbed his whiskered face, like it was a snare skin. "You think he could blow with the LB sound?"

"Art got a tough style," Felt said.

"Yeah, but it ain't LB style. Dizzy might do it, but you know that boy can't keep a secret."

"What about Don Byrd?" Felt asked. "He's alive and well, teaching college and shit."

"And playin that Donald Byrd Style," Red said. "Very much I'm sure. Hub, too. When those cats were young they sounded a lot like Lonnie, but they got their own sound now. And anyway, no one of that caliber is about to come up here and do a free date and then leave their name off."

"Who then?" Felton asked, lubricating his new reed and mouthpiece.

Red's thumb was shaking, hitchhiking toward me.

Felton lowered his jaw and let the La Voz soft-medium slide out. He had a good laugh. I laughed along. Red said he didn't know what was so funny.

"You play?" Felton asked me.

"A little."

"LB played more than a little," Felton clucked.

"Got that right," I said.

"Can't no woman—" Felton started to say. "What I mean...No offense to Chlora or nobody else...Or you, Miss Heron," Felton wheezed, "...but I ain't never seen no lady really dominate a horn."

"I guess I haven't either," I told him, though it did make me a little mad.

Red shook his finger at Felton. "You shouldn't a said that."

"Aw, come on," Felt replied.

"Drop it," I said. "It doesn't matter. No human being ever blew the trumpet like Lonnie Baylor and nobody ever will. Nobody had LB's soul, his power, his authority!"

"You could," Red insisted. "If you really wanted to."

And that really pissed me off. I said: "You've never even heard me play."

Felton laughed at that.

"Man, shut up," Red told him. "I don't need to hear her play. I know this lady. She woke me up to my life and that's soul. She turned my son around—that's authority. Power? Didi, you got power you don't even know about. And you forgot one other thing that made LB great—you got the love. Love of life and love of the music. You got that, Didi Heron. Got that as much as Lonnie ever did."

"But the chops, Red. I don't have the chops to play like that."

"That's just work—night and day, day and night. Ain't that right, Felt?"

Felton shrugged. Then flopped his head to the side, his eyes checking me out, staring at my chest. Probably trying to gauge my wind capacity. Maybe not. "Yeah," he finally said. "Maybe we could get you some chops."

I didn't know Felton well enough to tell if he was for real or just messing with me, so I accepted the offer with nonchalance.

Felton shrugged again and added: "What do you have to lose, lady?"

"I'll need a horn," I said. "I left mine back in New York."

Felton smiled a long smile. "I never thought..." he started to say.

An hour later, the three of us were in the rented Nova with Felton's new sax and Red's new kit. Felton sat in the backseat with his oxygen. I sat next to Red while he drove and read street signs to Felton who hollered directions at Red. Felton refused to say where he was taking us, only that I would end up with a horn. We wound up on the outskirts of New Haven, on a cinder and ash road breathing the corrosive air between a mountain of old tires and a boarded up, graffiti-covered factory. The road got bumpy and Red seemed to be aiming the car right at the big craters.

"Red! Slow down!" I cried, and Red slammed the brakes. The car skidded and kicked up dust. It poured in through the open windows.

"Let me drive," I said, coughing.

"No no. Uh-uh," Felton said. "This a band now. Band got to follow rules."

"Fuck that shit!" I said.

"Hey!" Felton said.

"How am I supposed to play like LB—how'm I supposed to cop that soul, power, and authority—if I can't even be allowed to drive a damn car?"

There was a long silence. Felton puckered, squinted, hiding his eyes, then mumbled: "Lady got a point."

Red seemed to be doing calculations in his head. Then he nodded, put the car in park, and got out so I could slide over. The mirrors were all crooked, like Red hadn't been using them. The seat was too close to the wheel. I adjusted everything, buckled up, and shifted into drive.

And I drove—like there was no argument who ought to be driving that car.

I wondered where the hell were we going and it pissed me off that I had to make my vehicular statement on such godforsaken terrain. But I managed, a delicate weave between craters and lumps, until Felton yelled, "Stop!" and pointed across a rock pile to what appeared to be an old cemetery. "Can't drive no closer."

I opened the door, stepped onto the uneven ground. I helped Felton out of the backseat with his oxygen tank. "Carry the tire jack and tools," Felton said.

"What for?"

"You'll see."

The stuff was heavy but I got inspired seeing Felton lug his own oxygen, refusing Red's offer for assistance. We moved slowly toward the cemetery crowded with tombstones, mostly crude rock, facing in all directions, leaning—some fallen on their sides. I supposed it was a pauper's graveyard, but didn't ask. I read the names of the dead—Holly Williams, Lester McDougal, Bradley Scott Jr.—like they ought to mean something. Felton stopped and stood beside a small, rough-hewn stone, a name crudely carved out. Red and I looked down at it. It said:

AX DAT MADE MUCH WAX
1947-1956

"Isn't it against the law to dig up a grave?" I asked.

"It ain't a person down there," Felton reassured me.

Red shook his head and stared off into the distance at the horizon of smokestacks and trees. "How'd you end up with it?"

"Man, I just did. Lonnie's mom. I visited her in D.C. couple months after the funeral. Woman was tore up. She said here you go. I said all right. Used to carry it around with that tape, thinkin I'd sell them to someone. Museum of Natural Sad History, maybe. If I ever need cash for my veins, you understand? Then, when I kicked, I didn't want money." He paused and took three hard breaths on the tube. "Still don't. So I buried it. Almost buried the tape, too. Might have maybe preserved it."

Felton rested his oxygen tank and reached over to me for the lug wrench which he used to dislodge the tombstone, surprising a family of worms who quickly burrowed deeper into the earth. I squatted and used the jack as a shovel. Red told Felton to relax and keep an eye out for the police or anyone else who might not understand what we were doing, then he took the wrench and stabbed the ground, loosening it for me.

About a foot down was an infant casket. It had rounded edges and a wood inlay of a half moon and some stars. Must have cost Felton some serious green at the time. Red and I reached down, got our fingers beneath it, and lifted, resting it gently on a bed of weeds. I got scared. What if Felton was just plain crazy and this wasn't LB's trumpet? Felton opened the lid. I closed my eyes, until I heard Red say:

"There it is. Man…"

I looked down—and there it was. The horn still shone, mangled as it was. Its mouth pipe was all bent and the valves all different heights, their casings dented. The tuning slide was folded up, the bell flattened and pointing down.

I reached for the instrument, picked it up, felt its weight, heard its silence. The mouthpiece was intact and I pushed it up against my lips.

"Blow," Felton said.

I shook my head. No way! Bad enough to see it, to touch it. I didn't want to hear what had become, sound-wise, of LB's instrument.

"Go ahead," Red insisted. "Got to hear it sooner or later."

I licked my chops, put them back on the piece. I blew for a middle C, and a sound emerged: middle C. A slightly pained but nevertheless full tone. Somehow all the flaws, the dents, the twisted pipe, all the deflection and detouring the air now had to make within the brass, somehow it came home to the right pitch.

I tried the valves. Dents and all, they worked. I opened the spit valve and blew, and thought the crazy thought of how much of the saliva was mine and how much was Lonnie Baylor's.

I took Felt shopping for clothes, toothpaste, the basics. My Alamode Mastercard still worked on purchases of less than $25. On the way back to the motel, we stopped at the clinic so Felt could ask Dr. Kaufman how long the oxygen tanks were supposed to last and how he could get more. Dr. Kaufman found two more and when Felton told him what we were doing, the doc got his colleague to donate that Teac 1000 to our cause and offered to open up the health center's employee dining room. Said he would invite patients and doctors for a night of bebop, a return to an evening in 1956—as soon as we were ready.

I spent the rest of that week familiarizing myself with LB's trumpet. I flexed my chops with scales, stretched out on some standards: *Stardust, Summertime, Too Young for the Blues*. Red showed me the way LB tightened his lip and how it made his forehead curl over his eyes. Felton showed how LB's nostrils would flare out when he paused. Interesting stuff but nothing that was going to help me rip out the Lonnie Baylor sound.

Felton talked to me on his tenor saxophone so that I could talk back on LB's trumpet. We chatted and argued musically and sometimes together we said something quite eloquent. We spoke low against strong evening breezes, and loud against anemic morning sunrises. Neighboring motel guests complained and a warning from motel management moved our musical conversations to a nearby park where nannies and mothers looked on; curiously, a few kids moved to the invisible beat, and birds flew wildly, as if in anticipation of an approaching storm.

I was in the room with Red when he telephoned Carlton Von Schmidt and talked him into making us a quartet. Red's last words, before he hung up, were, "You can afford the plane ticket. You got money, you cheap old mothafucka!"

Coming down the ramp at the New Haven Airport a few days later, hauling his bass which he'd bought seats for—Palm Springs to Denver, Denver to Philly, Philly to New Haven—Carlton seemed to be in shock. He had lost weight in his face and neck and gained in his belly. He greeted Red with a rigid handshake, did not say hello to me. "I haven't forgiven that girl for taking you away," he told Red. "Nor have I forgiven you for allowing her to." But Carlton was more than cordial toward Felton Payne, telling Felt how highly Red had always spoken of him, and then giving Felt a verbal resume of all the film and television scores on which he'd played and to which he'd contributed his musical ideas.

Carlton got his own room and complained about the price. Felt thought maybe the old white guy didn't want to cohabitate with black folks, but Red assured us that was not the case. Said Carlton's sleeping habits were peculiar, that he often arose in the middle of the night and needed room to pace and brood and needed light to see the way to his tranquilizers.

He bought himself a little portable record player and picked up some LB Five albums so he could study what Cole Anderson had going on. He did that at night and spent most of the days with Red on a landing above the second floor where Red set up his Pearl kit each morning. The two-man rhythm section practiced in the sun, during the hours when guests were gone and uniformed women busily cleaned the rooms.

One afternoon, Felton and I made it up there and the four of us jammed on the first couple tunes: the up-tempo *Morningside Drive* and *You've Changed*. We threaded up the faded reel of tape, listened hard, and then went outside and tried to recreate the exact phrasing and improvisation. Red picked up where he'd left off twenty years ago. Felton sounded heartier than ever as he blew between gasps from the o-tank. Even Carlton managed to hold his own, keeping the musical bottom together and improvising when called upon with a roundness that was a whole new him. Red took credit for it, said so at dinner one night in a coffee shop called The Pillar. He told us how he had acquainted Carlton with the recordings of Charlie Mingus—who, like Carlton, had started off as a classical cellist—and Jimmy Blanton and Paul Chambers on a phonograph back at Steiner Hall.

But Carlton wasn't having it. "Mingus?" he said. "Blanton? Chambers? Mere mortals of the instrument! I'm the first bassman!"

Red laughed. "Now you *really* startin to sound like Cole Anderson!"

What we didn't talk openly about was how I wasn't keeping up. Not even teasing at that Lonnie Baylor sound. And didn't have much time to get it together. Cash money all but gone and plastic Alamode bread now a sometime thing. I knew Red had a little money—I think Lou had stuffed a few bills in his pocket when he left—and cheap ass Carlton definitely had some cash in the lining of his suitcase. But I was determined to keep everything on the Alamode tab. Soon even dinner at The Pillar became an extravagance. We ate boloney sandwiches in our rooms most days, which left more time for work: listening to the in-and-out sounds of the original tape, transposing all the charts from that long ago date, and talking musical ideas and wondering where we would find the pianist to play on behalf of Billy Heron. We jammed together, sometimes whispering the music in Carlton's room, the strain of tight-lipped softness painfully adding a richness to my tone, especially when I let loose later at the park with Felton. But I wasn't quite sure what to do with the fuller inflection, how to express it and where to put it and where not to put it.

One night, I was shaken out of a deep sleep—electric mud sloshing round my brain. I heard Felton Payne shout in my ear: "Wake up!" Then his hand cracked me across the face. I made a fist and started to swing but before I could, Felton stuck the cold mouthpiece of LB's trumpet to my numb lips. "Blow!" he demanded.

My chops tightened and strained out an F-sharp that became an E-flat.

"Keep playing. Just play whatever is in your head."

I closed my eyes and tried to return to my dream, but it was gone, and I spat out the mouthpiece and said, "What the hell is this?"

"Thought it might help," he said.

"How did you get in here?"

"Technique I learned. Sorry to upset you. I just thought it would help. Lonnie used to have me do this at times."

"Break into his room and wake him up?"

"Lonnie wasn't too sure about himself."

"Uh-huh," I said skeptically.

"He had the splendidest sound, but you got to understand, he was not confident about improvising. Couldn't let loose 'cause he ain't had that confidence."

"This is Lonnie Baylor you're talking about."

"Is that strange?"

"Yes," I said. "You're talking about one of the giants of—"

"Boy had to make himself great. Had to get the freeness in his playing. Had to capture that spontaneous combustion."

"You for real?" I said.

"I'm for real," Felton said. "Genius ain't just something you can thaw out and heat up simple."

"I'm glad you told me that."

"That's good."

"But don't ever break into my room again."

He twisted his shoulders into a shrug and turned away. I fell back on my pillow and laid the horn on a chair next to my bed. "No, wait," I said. "All right. Do it. Break in here and wake me up with the horn. But don't slap me. Please don't ever slap me. Splash water on my face if you have to."

"You got it."

And I did get it. A cold wash cloth, then a cold trumpet. Every night. First few nights, I would rise and mime, pushing the valve buttons but not blowing. Hearing sound inside my head but not playing anything. Then I got to where I would play, but mostly what I played was atonal. It was spontaneous but it was nothing you'd call combustible. By the sixth night, I was anticipating the washcloth and woke up ahead of it and I blew hard and freely with absolute spontaneity into LB's horn—blew from the depths of my dreaming mind. No hesitation or thought. And at seven that morning we were told to vacate the Peat Motel.

We found a Quality Inn ($11 per night) about a half mile down Route 22, next to a colonial-styled fried chicken take-out which gave off a tantalizing 24-hour aroma. We couldn't risk being uprooted and relocated again, farther away from the health center, so Felton stuffed balled up socks inside LB's trumpet at night, allowing me to improvise with all my might. Blowing against the pressure of compressed fabric built fresh callous and muscle on my lips and, I think, helped to sharpen the edge of my embouchure. But when it was jam time—in the fried chicken parking lot or at a new park—I still wasn't producing any kind of sound that would convince any experienced jazz listener that it had come from Lonnie Baylor. Red and Felton seemed to know it, but didn't have the heart to say anything. I wasn't sure if Carlton could tell, until one morning when he invited me into his room for a word. The place stank of unwashed socks and pill bottle cotton.

"Look," he said, "you know I don't like you at all. But I want this to succeed. Red says it's important to him that we do this right."

"You gonna tell me something I don't already know?"

"You needn't get cross with me," he said. "Now listen. Despite my enmity for you, which is obvious and not entirely unjustified, I do believe it is not beyond possibility for you to achieve the stated objective."

"What the hell are you talking about?"

"How can I make it plainer than that?"

I reached for the door.

"All right," Carlton said. "Put simply..." he said, laying an icy hand on my shoulder, then quickly retracting it, then putting an entire boney arm across my back. "What I intend to say is, I'm with you. And if there's anything I can do..."

And I don't know why I cared what he thought or felt, but I did.

Felton and Dr. Kaufman set a date, ten days off. Felton told us the doc was excited about the idea. Patients and friends of the health center staff were being sworn to secrecy, though they weren't told exactly what we were doing.

"Man, I just don't know where we gonna find this pianist," Red said that night. We were all in Carlton's room sharing some cheese and crackers and a six pack of Kroger lemon lime soda. "Every musician a businessman these days. Nobody works for free. I even called that Berklee School up in Boston and nobody. Just nobody."

"That's good," Felton said. "That's good to hear. These young boys gettin' smart. Girls, too."

"Man," Red said, "never should have made definite plans until we knew."

"Had to," Felton said. "I added up the money and figured how long we got to go. Less you want to move it down 'neath the Merritt."

I went outside and walked. I saw Red behind me for about a block, then I didn't see him anymore. I kept going, down the street toward the Peat Swamp. A symphony of frogs were croaking. Just doing it. Doing what had to be done. Millions of them, it sounded like. Invisible to me and deafening, louder than the passing trucks on the highway. I could hardly think. I turned around and went back to the motel, to the payphone behind the swimming pool. The air was heavy with the smell of chlorine, insecticide, and deep frying oil. Mosquitoes skimmed over puddles near my feet. I kicked at them while I dialed Derrick's number.

He was home and recognized my voice right away, glad to hear it. "I'm doing well," he said, before I asked. "Clean for three months now. Working steady. Mostly pop studio gigs for Alamode. Making the money, playing good music. Best thing ever happened to me. Since you, I mean. So—why the call?"

I didn't answer.

"What?" he asked. "What is it?"

"Nothing," I said.

"I miss you, Didi."

"Yeah."

"We oughta have lunch.

And I almost left it at that, but I thought about the three old men back at The Peat Motel and for some reason had an image of all of them playing in the Basie Band, though I don't believe any of them (I know for sure Carlton never did anyway) played for The Count. "One more time," Basie said at the end of *April in Paris* and pulled the trigger on another four sensuous sumptuous bars. Then, "One more once," to detonate another four bars. So I didn't let it go. I asked Derrick, "Can I trust you?"

"For lunch?" he asked, in his usual stupid way.

"Beyond lunch, and even dinner. Can I trust you with a secret?"

"Hey, come on."

"Answer me!"

"Didi, always. And now especially. Yeah, you can trust Derrick Gamble."

I told him about our impending gig and Derrick got all excited—no hesitation, no thought—just couldn't get over the idea of working with the great Felton Payne and Red Young and me. Next afternoon he arrived by Greyhound in a sharp tan suit with a white silk shirt. His hair was picked out in the back and hung down like a bullfighter's mane, a steel eighth note sparkled in the left lobe and brought out the gray undertone of his sly brown eyes.

Red and Carlton and Felton stood behind me while I greeted Derrick from a distance. I could feel the eyes of the three men behind me, curious eyes, trying to read the situation.

When I gave D a stiff-armed handshake, he said, "It's gonna be like that?"

"You want to go home?"

Derrick looked past me. "You must be Red Young." He shook Red's hand. Red introduced him to Carlton. Then Derrick faced Felton. "Didi says you been clean a couple years. Me, I'm three months off that shit."

Felton said right on, and the two men embraced.

Derrick was traveling light. One small, tightly packed suitcase and a shoulder bag. In the parking lot, he offered to drive.

I started to hand those keys over. Back when we were together, Derrick had always done the driving, lousy driver that he was, mind always somewhere else. But I caught myself, held onto the keys, and told Derrick and everyone else, "We got rules in this band. No narcotics of any kind or any kind of serious drinking. Rule two: no selling charts to any other group. Three: no misbehaving of any kind, in the Fats Waller sense. Rule four: No men drivers!"

Derrick got his own room at the Quality Inn and invited me to move in. I told him, "No way." We were standing against the second floor rail between the two rooms. "I'm staying with Red."

"Oh," Derrick said. "You and Red? Him and you?"

"It's none of your business, is it, Derrick? And if we were, then, to quote Miles, 'So what?'"

"Cute."

"Yeah, well why don't you bunk with Felton? You can stay up all night rapping about your sobriety!"

Maybe I gave him more than he deserved. But I don't know—he deserved something. And the worst thing about his presence was the fact that his piano stylings, his underlines and elaborations, still moved me. Worse still was the possibility that Derrick Gamble on piano might have been just the thing

Didi Heron needed if she had any hope of elevating her sound toward an LB replication.

Derrick rented a Baldwin with his own funds and had it installed in the Peat Swamp Health Center cafeteria, and our quintet started practicing in the spot where we would perform.

Seeing me play LB's horn tripped Derrick out. He told me I did it justice but I didn't believe him. He listened to the faded, Sound Box recording—just one time—and then, I swear, he played *Morningside Drive* slow, then fast and with nearly the same precision and abandon my father had on his last night on earth.

"Boy can play!" Red and Felton declared within the first minute. Carlton said, "Not bad."

We ran through the entire first set, and Red was a new man on drums. On *Spontaneous Combustion* he went a little crazy and took about a ten minute solo. I was afraid it would kill him. But afterwards he seemed invigorated.

Carlton worked hard to keep up and did, for the most part, though he never really seemed to relax and I think that worried him, that he wasn't loose enough. He got together with Felton afterwards and they walked around the Health Center and the alley behind it talking and for the next few days they hung out in the afternoons. I didn't get nosey about it—though I did wonder, for a minute, if Carl had asked Felt to cop him some smack or something crazy. On my way to Rexall for some baby lotion I saw them next to a railroad bridge leaning over a row of trash cans, Carlton with a torn up Dairy Queen bag in one hand, a smashed box of Ritz crackers in the other. I never asked them about it but I got the feeling Carlton might have asked Felton for some kind of crash course in hunger and I did notice a change in him. More irritable but less fussy. The man got generous with his money, too, which helped us all get by those last few nervous wonderful days. He seemed to be feeling the music a little more, trusting his fingertips to make it happen, and I think that got us all in the same groove. It began to feel like we'd been a quintet for a long time.

Red thought we might get stale blowing that 1956 Soundbox lineup so many times, so we started messing around on standards—*Swingin' Till the Cows Come Home, Love You Madly, The Way You Look Tonight*—along with some of Felt's originals, some made up on the spot, like *Coughing from the Hallway*, and *Beautiful Nurses*, and *I Wish This Session Could Last for All Time*. We played whatever we could think of. Even made variations out of Carlton's own *Theme from the Outlaw Trail*.

Still, the day we were working for came too soon. Way too soon.

"I'm not ready," I told Red that morning in our room, and Red didn't say anything. He went out the door, came back sometime later with a jar of peanut butter and handed it to me. I opened the jar and ate some with my finger.

"Got to do it till you reekin from it, that's how LB did it," Red said, and I ate that peanut butter with a vengeance, like that was all I needed.

At 5:30, just before the audience would arrive for the dinner before the show, we checked our instruments. A sudden cooling trend had most likely changed the pitch on the piano and drums. Derrick and Red made some adjustments. Felton said that he and LB and Cole always tuned up in front of the audience so he and Carlton and I planned to do the same.

Dr. Kaufman met us along with his nephew, a shaggy-haired young man who, along with his friends, had built us the little stage we were about to perform on. He was going to operate the Teac 1000. Press the record button that was somehow supposed to turn it into a time machine. I clutched the old 3M box with trembling hands. The old box now contained fresh quarter-inch tape on a reel we had tossed around enough to make it look twenty years old. Red had to snatch it from me and give it to the guy.

I sat at the edge of the stage, my legs straight out, tapping against a metal chair in the first row of seats, and held LB's horn like a gun, closing my eyes and trying to imagine myself in three hours standing up on the unpainted plywood and blowing with authority. But all I saw was a mixed up montage of imaginary duets, my father and me, distant club dates and train rides hanging out with all the guys in Red's memories—and I wasn't sure any of that would do anything for me during the moment when I would actually have to play. I kept remembering how easily Nils Tanner had told me I didn't have it—which reminded me of something. According to some jazz aficionado, Bird had once said, *"If you don't live it, it won't come out of your horn."*

Felton and Dr. Kaufman were behind me, on the stage, figuring out where to set Felton's oxygen tank during the show, then talking about what Doc would say as MC. "Dude said, 'I want to welcome everyone to The Sound Box. I'm Harry Ragsdale, but the boys just call me Rags.'"

Kaufman cringed. "I have to say that?"

"And mean it," Felton said with a big laugh.

Soon we were all in the kitchen, waiting for our audience. Peeking out I watched men and women in white and green gowns. Couldn't entirely tell the patients from doctors and nurses, which I guess is the way it should be in a jazz club. There was a happy mood out there. Big excitement. Cranberry juice was served in wine glasses. I closed my eyes and listened and tried to imagine it was The Sound Box, Baltimore, 1956. I smelled the chocolate cake Felton Payne snuck between tokes on his oxygen tube, and I supposed that chocolate smelled about the same now as it had twenty years ago. I opened my eyes and saw Felt scarfing it down. Red was eating pieces of American cheese and seemed to be lost in far-away thoughts. Carlton smoked a cigarette out the back door. Derrick sat in a corner, cracking his knuckles.

Time came, and Dr. Kaufman took the microphone. He prepared the audience, told them to play it casual. "We're all cool cats from the Fifties," he said. Then he signaled for the tape recorder to start. He said his piece as Harry Ragsdale, and as he introduced each musician, we took our places: "Drummer Red Young, bassist Cole Anderson, pianist Billy Heron—owes me twenty dollars from poker last night...Ha ha! The incomparable Felton Payne on the tenor saxophone! And the living legend on trumpet: my man, Lonnie Baylor!"

I stood alone in the kitchen doorway, trying to believe it was me he was talking about, then stumbled onto the stage and fell into a bow for the audience. I was dizzy and a little nauseous. I kept thinking there was no fucking way I could pull this off.

Felton put the oxygen tube in his nose, then he and Derrick had a brief musical conversation, notes that seemed to be asking one another what tune to play. Heads in the audience bopped. A man in the front row gave us a toothless grin. Red crashed in on drums and Carlton strutted that bass line. I lifted LB's horn to my face and held it there, as if waiting for the brass instrument to play itself or for Lonnie's spirit to inhabit my body. But neither of those things happened. I watched Felton get into it, saw him look over at me, wondering if this was going to work. I felt the irrevocability of my failure. Then I looked over at Derrick, at his hands dancing across the white and black keys, and I found myself thinking about those fingers, where they would go next and what shape they would form. Then I felt the instrument in my hand and against my lips and I blew. I blew a long hollow B-flat into the musical tunnel, then, without breath, dropped it an octave beneath the surface and burrowed into the lower register of *Morningside Drive,* a musical place I could navigate in darkness. Red shook the room with some following syncopation and I saw, on his face, the recognition that I was right on, that he believed with twinkling eyes and without a doubt that pure LB was speaking now in soaring harmonies.

I closed my eyes and saw the music the way the horn wanted it played. Dreamt the melodies and then woke with a start for each solo. I moved step-wise, centrifugally from each melodic idea, savored each harmonic nuance to the bone.

I tasted the peanut butter in the music and I poured some sweet, succulent E-flat gravy out of LB's horn, one last time. We were jamming, and I mean everyone. Billy, my dad, was there. Him and LB and Cole—one last time and forever.

I had no idea what it was sounding like, until later, after the gig, after our audience was long gone and lights were low and we sat on the stage and listened to the tape.

"Man," Red said, in the pop and crackle between *How High The Blue Moon* and *Later Crocodilia,* "Billy Heron was really on that night.

"So was Red Young," I said, and he smiled.

"So was LB," Felton said.

"Amen," said Red, and then Derrick, and then Carlton.

Chapter Thirteen:

That Lonnie Baylor Sound

"Do you have an appointment?" Nils Tanner's secretary asked, the next morning, when I approached his office.

"Just tell him Didi is here."

A moment later Nils was standing in front of me. He wore a goatee and a grave expression. "We have to talk."

"Wrong," I said, holding up the flat 10-inch box. "We have to listen."

To a white guy in a dashiki strolling down the hallway, Nils said, "Taber, come thread this up for me." Once in his office, Nils opened the box and cradled the reel in his thumb and index finger for a moment. Finally, he handed it over and allowed his assistant to thread the leader through the heads and onto the take-up reel of a sparkling Nagra built into the wall like a safe. Nils showed me where to sit. He smiled over the box in his hand, delighted and amazed. He found the thin cardboard with the faded lineup of tunes and held it up and shook his head over and over. "Where did you find it?"

"In an attic," I told him because Felton Payne had told me he wanted to remain dead to the world.

"An attic," Nils repeated. The disbelief in his voice sounded like awe but I couldn't help wondering if there was a touch of skepticism.

"Not Red's sister like we thought. His son's ex-wife used to live in Connecticut, just outside New Haven. She still owns the house but rents it out. That's why it took so long. The people didn't want to let us up."

"Wow!" Nils shook his head again. "Crazy."

Seemed like Taber was having trouble with the capstans on the new machine. Nils told him to be careful, take his time. The silence got large and made me nervous. I thought, suddenly, there was no way this tape was about to fool anyone, least of all these folks. "What's the problem?" I asked Nils, to get his eyes off me, and he looked over at Taber again, but just then the crackling pops of the tape filled the speakers around us. Taber sat down and watched Nils, who hung on every word of the intro, mumbled, "I can't believe this," probably just a figure of speech but in my nervous state I almost blurted out a confession.

The opening chords of *Morningside Drive* shook the room and Nils braced himself. Hearing the tenor sax, he said, "There's Felton Payne. My, can he scramble those eggs!"

"Right on," Taber agreed.

"Where's Lonnie Baylor?"

"I believe Lonnie comes in after a few bars," I said.

And in I came—and Nils' head shook, back and forth, back and forth, with the beat, thank God. Not a judgment but a confirmation. His head kept time and his eyes were open as he concentrated on the music. Then, on about the third bar of my solo, the shaking of his head left the beat. Now he was making a statement about what he was hearing.

I wanted to know what, but was afraid to ask.

Nils waited until the trumpet solo was finished, then said, "Nothing like it. That Lonnie Baylor sound!"

"Nothing like it," I repeated.

Nils leaned back and grooved. He beamed through the entire first set and most of the second. Closed his eyes like he was trying to imagine The Sound Box, 1956.

Just for fun, I closed my eyes and imagined the Peat Swamp Health Center cafeteria, 1976.

On *Now's The Time,* Nils opened his eyes. "Man! They did a whole new thing with that. It sounds almost avant-garde but it really never fully departs from the flavor of the original. Remarkable. Some of those other tunes, I've never heard them before—by anyone else. Or maybe I just I don't recognize them."

He held up the tune list and mouthed the names with awe. *Now's The Time* gave way to applause and then *That Lonnie Baylor Sound.* I told Nils what was on the other side of the hand scribbled musical program. He flipped the list and looked at the tickets. His mouth fell open. "That's going on the liner notes," he said. "A photo of the ticket and an explanation." Then he set the thing gently on his desk and listened to my recreation of the LB sound signature. "There'll never be another LB. The emotion, the tenderness, the strength, the tragic joy."

When the reprise of *Morningside Drive* came on, Nils said, "That was Billy Heron's tune. Man, listen to him play. You're right, he was just coming into his own as a pianist that night."

"Don't rip them off," I said. "Give them a fair price."

"Them?"

"Red Young, his family."

"What does he want?" Nils asked.

"Twenty-thousand dollars," I said.

Nils raised an eyebrow. So did Taber. Nils said, "Twenty thousand!"

Taber laughed. "We'd be lucky to break even at eight!"

Nils didn't give a crap. He said, "Make it sixty." He seemed drunk—though I guess in a way what he was saying was really quite sober. He said, "The parent company of this company is not a parent at all. Last week we signed Hot Pants Funk Experience for a quarter-mil!"

With the money for the release of the lost (now found) tape split three ways, Red, Felton, and Carlton got themselves a three bedroom apartment in Lou's building in Port Clay. Red sent me a postcard with their new address and phone number. He described Carlton's hatred of Ohio, but how he was also slowly getting to like it. Lou and Anya sent regards. I missed everyone. I even missed Carlton. I especially missed Red, driver of the time machine on which I still wanted an occasional ride.

I knew I'd get over it, but wasn't sure I wanted to.

I got busy collaborating with Nils on the release of the album. I convinced him to let me write the liner notes and assisted the research department in double checking who composed each tune. Advance orders were good. For a jazz album, anyway.

Derrick Gamble still wouldn't leave me alone. He managed to find excuses to drop by Alamode whenever I was working there and urged me to get back into playing my horn—offered me a spot in his combo—but I preferred to remember my splendid performance rather than have to live up to it. I was afraid it had been a fluke.

One morning Derrick cornered me at Alamode and wouldn't move till I agreed to go to lunch with him. When I refused anyway and snuck around him, he went to a window, as if threatening to jump, though the windows in that building did not open.

"I was always a jerk," he told me. "That magical great guy Derrick you remember is bullshit. I'm the real Derrick."

"Thanks for the insight," I told him. "Now I *know* I don't want to go out with you."

"Please!" he begged. "Just on a date. Let's start over with some honesty about ourselves."

"Get out of here," I said over and over, until he did, and then I went after him. He was my only reminder of those great days of the reunited reincarnated LB Five. And he was the living musical extension of my father, Billy Heron. In that regard, I was basically a hostage.

"I'll go out with you," I said, "but don't get your hopes up."

LB's birthday—October 8th—was approaching and the *One Last Time* LP was rushed out to capitalize on the coincidence. I checked Sam Goody one afternoon and discovered that it was on the racks two days early. I strode up to the small cardboard display—a faded image of Lonnie Baylor surrounded by smoke and the words *LB Lives!*—at the front edge of Goody's jazz section and I picked up a copy. I was excited. My first time on vinyl!

In the coming weeks I did some live radio promotion, mostly public FM stations, mostly by phone. But I did fly back out to L.A. to go on KBCA, that 24-hour jazz station with DJ Sam Fields. I told him about my adventures tracking down the tape. I guess I was suffering from jet lag because I slipped up: when Sam asked me to tell the listeners where I'd found the tapes I said: "In a garbage dumpster…" But then I caught myself and added: "Metaphorically speaking."

"Metaphorically speaking," Sam repeated. "We can certainly dig that." Then he cued up some choice cuts for the So-Cal listeners—*Conjunctive Moonbeams, You've Changed, Morningside Drive*—and we rapped about how great the music was, what a tragedy that car accident had been and how not one but two jazz legends were taken from us.

We closed the interview with *That Lonnie Baylor Sound.* Sam's ultra mellow introduced it: "LB with his legendary quintet: Felton Payne on the tenor, Billy Heron piano, Cole Anderson Bass and Red Young on the drums. Though on this tune it's mostly just LB and the spirits, you might say. One of the most awesome eight minutes of trumpet playing I've ever heard."

"Yeah," I couldn't resist agreeing, "no other sound quite like it."

Downbeat devoted a cover and a big article to the release and an entire issue to the brief but brilliant career of Lonnie Baylor and to the careers and achievements of Red Young and the late Billy Heron and Cole Anderson and the [still-officially] late Felton Payne.

Sales of the LP were impressive, making my dinner out with Derrick a celebration of our success. Derrick arrived at my apartment forty-five minutes early with a bouquet of lilies. He wore a shiny indigo suit he said one of his rehab buddies had sold him along with a white shirt and cobalt necktie. Took me to Victor's on the Westside for *paella* and some reminiscing—remembering our LB Five days in Connecticut, like it really *was* years ago. He showed me the *Downbeat* thing like I didn't already know and showed me how we had the #1 selling jazz album in France and Japan.

After dinner, he took me to see that Broadway show everyone was talking about—*A Chorus Line* and, yeah, it had some swing and a lot of heart. It was cool to see something like that, a theatrical revolution for our time. Derrick thought we should write the jazz version: a rhythm section and some horns, on stage playing and talking about themselves. He told me this idea after the show at The Russian Tea Room. He was drinking lemonade after insisting I drink this very expensive wine that was now giving me a headache.

"You all right?" he asked me.

"Not really."

"Wine didn't agree with you?"

"It's you. You don't agree with me."

"Come on, Didi. You said you'd give it a chance. "

"I can't just start over and pretend I don't know you."

"Then what, Didi? What do you want from me?"

"Nothing, Derrick. I don't need anything from you and don't want anything from you." I looked him over: those mournful eyes and the same damn nose hairs he never got around to trimming, same slouching posture. That suit was sharp, but somehow didn't look right on him, like a con dressing up to appear in court. I leaned over the table to give him a consolation kiss. Derrick met me halfway, over the candle, so that his tie began to smolder. But he didn't care. His kiss roused me like it always had, like the first fingerings of one of his really hot piano riffs.

Downbeat and *Playboy* came out with their top ten jazz albums and we were on both lists. I got a call from Nils, congratulating me and offering me an official job at Alamode. He said I would be working my way in with a bunch of departments—marketing, research, new artist development—and would be heading up a new department unearthing lost jazz treasures. Sounded good, especially the last part, though I felt a little silly pretending to be an expert on something I'd only accomplished fraudulently. Derrick encouraged me to take the job. He said he might have some leads for me on a tape of Lee Konitz blowing his tenor in the bathtub, and a session D referred to as Dizzy with Curly Russell in Outer Space and another of Lee Morgan playing ballads for prison guards at Rikers. Still, I just wasn't sure I wanted to be any kind of record label executive.

Then I got a call from Red. I asked him if he'd seen those top ten lists and, to my amazement, it was all news to him. Felton and Carlton, too. Only thing any of them wanted to talk about was some music they were working on. Red said, "Man, we got us a new sound. This time it's for real. A whole new progression in music. So obvious, nobody's seen it coming. I can't explain it." He put Felton on the phone to explain. Felt's voice was low and strained: "Whole thing 'bout music is something you write down, and then anyone can play it and maybe change it up here and there—that's an old idea." Felton paused, and I imagined he was sucking his oxygen tube. "But the idea that you just freeform it, that's old, too. Ornette and Trane and many other cats already done put that shit in the pocket many years ago. So what's new is where the music and the place where it's happening come alive together. Not just the way an audience affects you on a stage..." Long breath. "But the way the environment of the music helps to create the music. Like when I was out there living under the Merritt, my music changed. I played what I heard and what I saw, and here in this very nice pad overlooking this Great Lake, and hearing a refrigerator humming, the freezer making ice. What I'm saying is..."

Suddenly, Carlton was on the line. "What he's saying is that we live in an age in which we're bombarded with sensorial images and we must recognize that they are at the very essence of the creative process."

There seemed to be a struggle on the other end for possession of the phone. "Hello?" I wasn't sure who, if anyone, was there now. Then one voice emerged:

"Didi, you there?"

"Red?"

"Yeah, so what do you think? I mean, we oughta play somethin for you, but in the meantime..."

"Sounds exciting. Sounds promising," I said. A generous assessment of something I hadn't actually listened to—and even if there was something to what those guys were doing, musical innovation just doesn't get much appreciation, not right away. Still, after everything we'd been through, the insincerity of my encouragement had a stale aftertaste that lingered on my tongue long after I said goodbye. Next day I called Nils and told him I'd take the job. He said I could start any time.

So I started the next day. I was nervous. Spent an hour figuring out what to wear and how to wear it. Settled on jeans and a plain T and brought in LB's trumpet, in its battered case, as a good luck charm—and a weapon, I guess—then got worried something would happen to it so I locked it up in a file cabinet. I didn't do much. After a few days everyone pretty much forgot about me. Now and then someone would ask me to listen to a demo of something and give an opinion but otherwise I was left alone. I waited a week before I approached Nils and told him about Red and the fellows and their new sound. I tried to convey it to him the way Red and Felton and Carlton had told it to me. I wasn't sure I did it justice, or whether I could have; it sounded pretty nebulous and more than a little nutty. "I think you should give them a contract," I said.

"Hey," Nils said. "Red is my man. I told him I thought he and that other gentleman showed promise. I'd love to hear what they're up to."

I shook my head. "No, just give them a record deal."

Nils grinned incredulously. "Didi. Are you telling me how to run this label?"

"I'm telling you that Red and his friends are too old to be waiting around for you to make up your mind. You're not going to like it anyway—you know you won't—and it shouldn't be about that, not for them, not now. I'm telling you that you need to give them a contract. Not a big one. Just something. Some kind of recognition for what they're doing now."

"Didi, we're running an entertainment company. We have a procedure. There's a decision-making mechanism at the GLX family. We don't just throw money at people!"

"Make an exception. Do it or I'm going public with the truth."

"We're all about the truth: musical and otherwise," Nils said.

"Felton Payne is alive and living outside Cleveland, though he was in Parkside Connecticut when we found him. He recreated his performance. Twenty years later. So did Red Young on drums. The bassist was not Cole Anderson. The pianist was in diapers when my father died."

"Felton Payne is alive?"

"He had the tape in the pocket of his trench coat which I fished out of a garbage dumpster. The tape had pretty much forgotten what was recorded on it."

"Wait a minute. Felton Payne? The late great Felton Payne?"

"Late great is only half-true. He's working with Red on their musical breakthrough. So give them a contract."

"That album is a fake?"

"It's the musical truth—as you say—but otherwise..."

"Felton Payne. And is Lonnie Baylor *also* still alive?"

"Musically speaking?"

"Stop fucking with me, Didi. Is the man who goes by the name of Lonnie Baylor walking around and breathing?"

"No."

"Then who played trumpet? Who blew that Lonnie Baylor sound?"

I walked out of the office, went back to my office, opened the file cabinet and pulled out LB's horn. I came back to Nils and held it up. He seemed puzzled for a moment, then he just stared at it and muttered: "Oh, my God."

I put the instrument to my lips and blew. I wasn't sure I could generate that Lonnie Baylor Sound again after more than eight weeks, but I didn't hold back: I blew the opening five bars from *That Lonnie Baylor Sound*.

And blew Nils Tanner away.

"You had no right, Didi," he said.

I answered the charge with the next five bars. When I lowered the horn, Nils had fire in his eyes.

"You defrauded me. You've put this company in a position where we could lose our credibility. I could be personally humiliated in the industry!"

"Nobody has to know."

Nils shook his head with disgust. "Don't get cocky with me. I could ruin you. And I ought to." Then he stormed out of his office and left me to wilt in my chair, resting the trumpet on my lap.

He returned in what seemed only a few minutes, and said, "You're fired." And handed me a typed piece of paper. I tried to read the top paragraph but nothing made sense.

"What's this?" I asked.

"A memo."

"Saying I'm fired?"

"No, I'm firing you with God as my witness. The memo says your friend Red and whichever individuals he's working with—dead or alive—have been contracted to produce one album, untitled, for the Alamode label, of, can I call it, progressive jazz?"

"Yes, progressive jazz. Wonderful," I said.

"Not so fast. There are two very important conditions."

"Is this a negotiation?"

"It's an ultimatum," Nils said. "That Mr. Young uses you as his trumpet player." He rose from his chair, reached down, and snatched LB's horn from off my lap. "That you give me this piece of jazz history, get your own horn, get your own style—and become what you were always meant to be."

Larry Strauss digs East and West Coast jazz and everything in-between, as much as his wife, Eleanor, and their three children—Nora, Carly and Sean—can stand. He is the author of three previous novels—*Fake Out*, *Unfinished Business*, and *One Man One Vote*.

Discussion questions for book clubs or classrooms:

Discuss Didi's insecurities as a musician. How does she ultimately confront them?

Didi embarks on the search for the lost tape as an homage to her father, but how much is she motivated by the distraction from her own personal disappointments?

Contrast the reactions of Red and Felton to the tragic loss of their musical leader, Lonnie Baylor. In what ways have they taken divergent paths? In what ways have their lives since the tragedy mirrored one other?

In chapter thirteen, *Embraceable Spirit*, Didi recalls something Charlie Parker once said: "If you don't live it, it won't come out of your horn." Why is this statement so important to her?

Explore the love/hate relationship Didi and other characters in the novel have with the music business.

Is commerce necessarily corrupting to the purity of music? Is the selling of music inherently a sell-out?

Consider the manner in which individual and collective memory, including musical memory, plays in the story.

The chapter titles all turn out to be the titles, in order, of the tunes on the lost recording, but how does each title directly or ironically relate to its chapter?

Is Didi's great performance a fairy tale? Consider the validity of what the man at the bar in chapter one says about the unlikelihood of a woman ever being a great horn player. Is that a reasonable assumption based upon jazz history? In the decades since this story takes place there have been many good women horn players, but no great ones—or is that just a matter of subjective opinion?